CALIFORNIA DREAMS CHRISTMAS ROMANCE COLLECTION

FIVE HEARTFELT, STEAMY LATER-IN-LIFE
SHORT STORIES

CALIFORNIA DREAMS SERIES

TALYA BLAINE

CONTENTS

INTRODUCTION FROM THE AUTHOR

As I was writing the first volume of forthcoming California Dreams series novelettes, for some reason I kept imagining the characters at Christmastime.

All that daydreaming about a warm, sunny Christmas in California, picturing iconic and imaginary places decked out in surfing-Santa decorations and romantic holiday lights gave me an idea: To write a collection of standalone short stories—sexy, sweet Christmas romances set in the Golden State.

And as soon as I committed to writing the collection, I had one of those *a-ha!* moments: Several cities in said state have "Santa" in their name. It was a match that could only be made in . . . well, California.

The characters and the places in the five stories in this collection are different from those in the forthcoming *California Dreams* novelettes. But just like in the novelettes, each contemporary romance in this short-story collection opens with a sexy dream.

Over the years I've come across plenty of writing advice that says authors should never start a story with a dream.

This author begs to differ. The dreams were So. Much. Fun. to write, and early readers said they loved reading them. Often, the dreams took twists and turns that surprised me, providing insight into the issues a character was struggling with. The dreams shaped the stories in ways I hadn't planned.

Speaking of twists and turns, all of the characters in these five stories are over 40, with some closer to the big 5-0. So they've been knocked around a bit by life. They might be professionally established and accomplished, but they've seen their plans and relationships move in directions they couldn't control or hadn't expected or didn't feel equipped to deal with. That, for me, is the most exciting part of meeting these people on the page—watching how they move forward.

Without spoiling any surprises, you'll meet a SoCal baker-to-the-rich and famous, the owner of a winery in the rugged Santa Cruz Mountains, a social worker playing Santa at a Santa Barbara nursing home holiday party, a grieving rebel-Santa in a biker jacket, and an aging (but still hot) B-list actor with a penchant for, shall we say, wish fulfillment.

Enemies to lovers, stuck in an elevator (or luxury beachfront vacation rental), second chance, fake relationship, friends to lovers, destined to be together—you'll find twists on common romance tropes in these pages. And you'll find a few themes that wove themselves throughout the collection: hope and healing, the willingness to laugh (at humor that's sometimes dark), the courage to be vulnerable, to try again, and the holiday spirit.

Humor and bravery bring these characters gifts that can't be wrapped or set under a tree—not only laughter but also forgiveness, self-acceptance, great sex. And, by the way, it's not only Santa doing the giving. Some of the Santas in these stories have wounds of their own that need help from our heroines to heal.

I hope you enjoy reading these stories and meeting these characters as much as I did writing them!

XO,
Talya

SANTA & ANNA

I n the dream, she was skating a wide figure-eight, arms stretched out like wings, gliding free. Cool air rushed past her face; her cashmere scarf fluttered. Blake and the kids waved from the far side of the huge rink, not far from the enormous tree. It might be Rockefeller Center on Christmas Eve, but somehow the four of them had the ice to themselves. Thousands of tiny golden lights adorned the skyscraper spruce, glittering like stars in the Manhattan twilight—indigo, fuchsia, and violet, backlighting the winter sk . . .

With a loud metallic crack, the blade of her skate broke clear off, sending her tumbling down to the ice. She spun on her back like a top, careened into the side wall with a thud.

The kids raced over. Blake took his sweet time.

"What happened?" he asked when he finally reached them.

"I fell," she started, but got distracted by the bottom of her bladeless skate, trying to understand what happened. There were no holes, no metal plates, no sign anything had once been attached.

"Yeah, I got that much, Anna." Arms crossed, he huffed six feet above her, his lips chapped and dry from the cold. He looked around for the kids, who were safely out of earshot now. "Enough with the sarcasm. We're not married anymore; you don't have to be a bitch."

And then—thank you, Christmas miracle—he disappeared. A rink security guard skated over and helped her up, dusted her off. The bell on the tip of his floppy green and yellow elf hat jing-a-linged as he moved.

Once she collected herself and got a good look at the man under the hat, she realized it was quite nice watching him in motion. The muscles of his chest and biceps flexed under his tight black sweater. His thick dark hair bounced. Heat stirred in her, somewhere deep and low. The space between them hummed with electricity; the air no longer felt cold. His blue eyes sparkled like a tropical lagoon, and they stayed fixed on her when he asked, "Can I take you home?"

Only it wasn't her Costa Mesa townhouse they went to, it was the back room of her bakery, with the order board on the wall, the tall racks of cooling pans, steel counters lined with waiting boxes, Anna's Bakery of Cookies printed on each lid. He spied the couch in her office, picked her up and carried her over the threshold, asked if he could stay.

She looked into the mirror beside the office door to see if this was real. The reflection was hers alright—brown eyes, roasted chestnut curls, hips whose curves gained extra padding this time of year. He stood behind her, started to unwrap her scarf as if she were a present, pressed his lips to her neck for a single kiss.

"Is this okay?" he wanted to know.

"Yes," she told him, leaning back against his broad chest. The bell on his hat jingled while he kissed his way down her body, until she accidentally knocked it off as she moaned.

———

ANNA WOKE to her phone jingling on the nightstand—Carli often changed her ringtone as a joke. Sadly, the images in the dream dissipated in the early morning sunlight streaming through the blinds. Blake being an asshole was not far from reality, but that she would finally have amazing sex with a gorgeous, sweet guy? *That* was about as likely in real life as Santa coming down her chimney. No pun intended. She did not have a romantic prospect to save her life. Or, for that matter, a fireplace.

When she turned over the phone, she discovered the kids had texted from New York. Ben sent her a photo of an amazing department store window display, one of the vignettes of a serious elf-bakery operation. Carli sent a selfie modeling a not-so-appropriate-for-a-sixteen-year-old dress. Blake's thumb cut into the corner of the photo, right by the exorbitant price tag. He had probably turned it around to make sure Anna would see it. It wasn't paranoia on her part; that was his MO.

Fine. Let him try to earn the kids' respect by buying them expensive stuff. She would not get aggravated over him. As she kept reminding herself since he picked Carli up last week to visit Ben at NYU, he was giving the kids a nice winter vacation, doing Christmas in New York. A picture-perfect, postcard-ready Christmas in Manhattan with his pretty, young new wife—"new" referring strictly to the recency of the wedding itself, not how long they had been screwing behind Anna's back.

After a plateful of scrambled eggs, she drove to her

shop. She would need the high protein start; Christmas Eve was her longest day of the year. Twelve-plus hours until she could take off her double-breasted white jacket, untie her apron, wash the flour out of her hair. And then she planned to do nothing more than fall onto the couch and binge-watch sappy movies. Romantic comedies with reliably happy endings, it was her guilty pleasure. She had been squirreling them onto her DVR since Thanksgiving.

By seven a.m., the bakery was buzzing with customers and her loyal skeleton holiday crew, with backup from seasonal temps. A line of patrons snaked around the glass cases piled high with colorful treats and curled out the front door. In the back, her team filled the large orders as mixers whirred and baking sheets clanged.

The day whizzed by, and the courier service took off in the delivery van at four o'clock. Her employees shouted Merry Christmas as they scattered, off until the twenty-sixth.

Anna locked the front door, turned the sign to closed. The extra-special orders were ready to go, including the big one for the hospital. She only had to load the stacks of the signature lemon-colored boxes in her Clubman, parked in the alley outside the back door.

This was her thing, every Christmas Eve, hand-delivering special orders to her best clients, nestled snug in their cliffside Coast Highway homes. Actors and politicians, surgeons and philanthropists, influencers and socialites. And just like Anna knew they didn't wear the same outfit to more than one event, she never made them the same cookies twice.

With the exception of the children's hospital, to which every year she happily donated hundreds of cookies, her clients paid handsomely—for her time, her creativity, her dependability, her reputation. They referred their friends and colleagues often. Without them, Anna's Bakery of Cookies wouldn't have grown from nothing to thriving these last few years of her rocky, post-divorce life.

She propped open the back door, piled up three boxes on the metal counter and shimmied the stack onto her forearms. Three at a time was her limit, her rule; she would not risk dropping them by trying to carry more.

She stepped outside, the late afternoon sun dipping below the rooftops. She set the boxes on the cargo floor, turned them so the short sides rested against the grate behind the front seats. It would be getting dark soon, but the angle of the light was sharp. Iced cookies, rays of sun, the car window a focusing prism. She hurried around to the driver's side to blast the A/C.

The radio came on when she pressed the ignition. "Traffic and weather up next," a deep practiced voice said, although she didn't wait to hear the report. The traffic she would check on her phone, and after the deliveries, she was going home. A shower, yoga pants. TV. She might shift positions to reach the Chinese food takeout containers or to exchange goodnight texts with the kids, but otherwise her plans were weather-proof.

The wind gusted warm and dry as she headed back toward the door. The Santa Anas were starting to blow. The hem of her chef's jacket fluttered, and her eyes squeezed shut to protect from a flurry of flying dust. Once inside, she slid the rubber doorstop out of the way with her foot, swapping it for a weighty bag of flour.

Her phone buzzed with a text alert, and she slid it from her pocket. A photo from the kids on the ice at Rockefeller Center, Ben giving Carli a noogie, the two of them grinning in front of the tree. For a moment, she thought of the hunk at the rink in her dreams, of the elf hat that jing-a-linged when she came.

The phone buzzed its second alert, and she tried to think of what to write. Upbeat-mom was the tone she strived for, rather than bitter-at-Blake that she and the kids were apart.

Fun!! she texted back. *Is it cold?*

Six boxes left on the counter, and the time was 4:29. She should hustle if she was going to deliver like she promised. It was only a few feet from the back door to the car—she could carry them all, make an exception this one time.

The phone buzzed again. Probably another photo from the kids, on their way to some famous place for a cup of hot cocoa. She could see in her mind's eye the glistening hand-whipped cream, the flecks of chocolate shavings, the dusting of cocoa powder—styled and social-media ready.

She bent her knees so her forearms were counter-height, shimmied the boxes forward. Carefully, she rose and went outside. The wind gusted again and she turned her face away. A few doors down some guy dressed as Santa was walking fast, his big belly jiggling, his head angled down toward his phone.

The wind gusted once more, noisily, and it was hard to tell, but it sounded like Santa yelled *fuck.*

The impact knocked her back, but she caught her balance and didn't fall. The long boxes—they were a different story. In slow motion, the top three angled forward. She leaned back to rein them in. But they had the advantage of momentum, and she winced as one by one they hit the sidewalk. The crushed lids bounced off, and cookies, broken cookies, spilled out.

"Sorry! Sorry! Are you alright?" Santa was asking as she

yanked her arm from his grip. "Something blew into my eye."

"I'm not alright! Look!" She pointed to the ground. You're a real. . ." *Jerk! Asshole!* "I can't believe. . . Why weren't you watching. . . Geez, what kind of idiot runs around *outside on the street* in a Santa costume? Couldn't you change, like a normal person, when you get to your—" she waved her hand around frantically, uselessly—"your. . . destination?"

He tried to say something, but she raised her hand to silence him. "Rhetorical question."

He looked at her like she was nuts, which at least temporarily, she was.

"I'm really sorry," he said, looking at his fucking phone screen again. "I gotta' go."

Seriously? The guy slams into her, busts up her cookies, and he just. . . just waltzes off, goes on his merry fucking way?

Wow, this male specimen made Blake look like the real Santa Claus.

"I'm really, really, really sorry," he called over his shoulder as he continued his saunter down the street.

Did he not learn anything just now? "Watch where you're going!" she screamed into the wind.

Reason edged into her thoughts. It was an accident. He seemed genuine when he said he was sorry. But his face had been buried in . . . probably some porn on his phone. He hadn't been paying attention, and instead of helping her fix the problem he caused, he left her standing here, cookies broken, alone.

Although, "cookies" technically was not the right word to describe the bits and crumbs scattered on the sidewalk like snow.

BREATHE. Inside the bakery, she set the three remaining boxes down on the metal counter to take stock. The boxes themselves were dented where she must have tightened her grip but—her body tensed as she lifted the lids—by some miracle, most of the cookies were intact.

Okay, come up with a plan. Prioritize. The hospital's Christmas party had already started, and soon the kids and their parents would expect dessert. From these boxes and the ones already in the car, she could salvage the hospital's order. There, part one: decided.

Then, she could hurry back here after the drop-off and re-bake the rest of the orders. She would call each client and explain. With any luck she'd only be a couple hours late.

Okay, not so bad. She could fix this. It was, actually, probably—no, it was totally—doable.

But. . . *No.* A sick feeling came over her, and she ran to the mixing area, slid back the top of the storage container that stood under the counter. A few tablespoons of white crystals framed the bottom of the sugar bin like snow in a windowpane corner.

The bakery was supposed to get a big delivery yesterday, but her distributor told her a Midwest snowstorm would delay it a couple of days. She had had enough on hand to bake her Christmas orders, but the shop had been so busy she forgot to run to the grocery store for her usual backup just-in-case reserve. That would be the grocery store that was now closed, like all the grocery stores within a reasonable driving radius.

Not once in eight years had she missed a delivery. Sure, there were mix-ups on occasion—like the time an employee had been high and put a bachelorette's extra-large penis cookies into a box destined for a confirmation. Anna never found out if it was a practical joke or honest mistake, but it was irrelevant. Errors were rare, relatively easy to apologize for and make amends. But today was Christmas Eve, and these were her top clients. The ones she didn't let down. The ones she couldn't afford to lose.

She would have to do major damage control to make up for this—deliver a bottle of top-shelf champagne, give them a year's worth of free cookies. If they came back. After the New Year, she would talk to the bank about a loan to cover operating expenses in case her revenue tanked.

She would have to let the clients know—call and grovel and explain. But first thing's first. Reshuffle the cookies into new boxes and get to the hospital stat.

THE CHILDREN'S hospital atrium had been transformed, a sparkling winter wonderland. Huge twirling snowflakes hung from the glass dome six stories high. Giant fake Christmas lights and ornaments in cheerful, bright colors dotted the North Pole scene amid tall, snow-capped evergreen trees. Directly underneath the dome, a large circle of fake snow glittered on the shiny floor. At the center sat a red and gold Santa throne, wide enough for two. A brigade of elves escorted the excited kids, first to Santa and then to his sleigh, piled high with gifts and surrounded by fake, life-size reindeer. Christmas carols filled the air, and some of the elves danced with patients waiting in line for Santa—and with their moms and dads.

The public relations director and her assistant spotted Anna and came over to say hello. One in a gorgeous red cocktail dress, the other in green, they led her to a long, decorated table set off from the hustle and bustle in the open area behind Santa's throne.

While they chatted, she hurried to arrange the cookies on the etageres she left with them last year. When she happened to glance up, an adorable little boy was hugging Santa, resting his head on the man's fuzzy red shoulder; the look on the child's face was pure joy.

Her heart warmed, then melted. Everything angry fell away. Blake, his perky wife, that moron Santa on the street. She might lose customers after tonight, but she had made the right decision. It was worth the consequences to help bring these kids even a little bit of holiday cheer, to have made them some special treats.

The PR director thanked her for supplying the cookies, smiled warmly, and put her hand on Anna's arm. "We'd love to get a few photos of you with the other donors and volunteers."

Quickly, Anna looked down to scan her outfit. Not great, but professional given her job and free of flour and food coloring. Under the rushed circumstances it would have to do: chef's jacket with her embroidered logo, smart wide-leg black pants, and—at least she had remembered to swap her clunky old clogs at the bakery's back door—her nice black ballet flats. "Come on," the director said, "I'll introduce you to Santa."

The three women chatted as they walked across the North Pole to the elves and Santa's throne. The last of the kids who had been waiting in line said goodbye to Santa and moved on to the sleigh to take a gift. The volunteer Santa stood and—

No. That full head of fake white hair, big bushy eyebrows that would make it hard to see, gold spectacles around vaguely familiar eyes that stared wide as saucers. *No, it can't be.*

The PR director was saying something about Santa's real name being James.

"Anna, I presume," he said, his gaze not leaving hers.

"Oh, you two know each other!" The director clasped her hands in delight.

"We've run into each other before," he replied as he turned toward her. "Anna, it's nice to see you again."

The anger that had melted away a moment ago flared back, and she resumed the fantasy she had nursed in the car. How she might—without causing serious, irreparable harm (it was Christmas Eve after all)—like to maim him. A swift kick to the jingle balls. A finger-jab to the base of the throat. Or, something—she couldn't recall the precise move —to do with the Adam's apple.

Wait, he was saying something to her—that must be why his mouth was moving. The PR director turned away to speak to someone else, while Santa kept on talking.

" . . . very sorry. I rushed off because I was late for the party, and you seemed really, like, steaming furious, and I—I know this is going to sound terrible—but I didn't have time to wait for you to calm down."

Oh, here it was. His leaving was her fault because she had been the angry woman, the bitch, the shrew. She slid her hand into her jacket pocket and felt the comfort of her phone. She would google that Adam's apple thing, find some detailed instructions so she could learn it pronto.

"I would have been furious in your shoes too," he continued, "but in that moment I had to make a choice— help you or get to the kids. I'm sorry; I picked the kids."

His words stopped her. Okay, maybe she could hold off on the web search.

"I haven't lived here that long, and I took a wrong turn—several wrong turns in fact. That's why I was in the alley; that's why I was using my phone. And then that damn gust of wind blew sand into my face. Anyway, I'm sorry again—clearly, I didn't see you until it was too late."

She should say something, but watching him speak, well, it was distracting. His eyes, his smile, they had a matching twinkle. Not a cliché romance novel twinkle, more like a bright, alert presence. A mature twinkle. Eyes that said, "I'm here." Eyes that maybe even held—despite how recent events might have appeared—a touch of kindness.

The photographer was corralling the group—elves in front, board members behind them, the PR staff flanking Santa. "Anna, you should be next to him, why don't you sit on his throne?"

His mouth formed a touch of a smile, and for some reason now it didn't aggravate her; it didn't strike her as smug.

He moved over as she climbed the three steps and sat down next to him, putting her elbow on the swirly gold armrest. While the photographer adjusted elf hats down in the front row, James turned to her. "May I?" he asked, his fingers in front of her forehead as if he were about to lift a wedding veil.

Right. The hairnet. Before she left the shop, she had forgotten to take it off. Her cheeks grew warm. "Sure. I can't believe I forgot."

Carefully he removed it, watched intently as her dark curls fell. Up close, she noticed his big hands, his long fingers, nails clean and nicely trimmed.

"You were busy cleaning up cookie crumbs," he said softly, that strange protrusion rising below his beard when he spoke. It was actually, well, when you saw it in the context of the rest of his face—the full, soft lips, the aquiline nose, that twinkle in his eyes—it could almost be construed as . . . sexy.

The photographer snapped away. Serious photos with the hospital CEO, silly photos of the elves, several shots of Santa and Anna to post on all their feeds. She let out a tense breath, and felt her shoulders loosen as they stepped down from the big chair together.

But her newfound sense of ease was short-lived as reality crept back in. She glanced at her watch. Like Cinderella at the ball, her time was running out. She could put it off no longer; she had to call those customers and break the bad news. A twin sense of dread and embarrassment rose in her gut.

"How bad was the damage?" he asked as they walked toward the table with her sweets.

She hesitated, wavering between total honesty and, surprisingly, not wanting him to feel worse. "It wasn't great, but—" she gestured to the nearly empty etageres—"I was able to salvage enough for the kids."

"But you had other customers?" he asked, stopping to look at her.

She nodded, and he immediately asked, "What are you going to do?"

A sigh escaped. "There's nothing I *can* do. I ran out of ingredients, and by the time I realized, the grocery stores were closed."

It hurt physically, although it was actually her pride, to say those words aloud. From day one, she had dotted every I and crossed every T. For every possible scenario, she had a policy, a rule, a backup plan—if not two.

And yet. A simple mishap and she had no solution.

"What are you missing?" he asked, his brow showing concern.

"This is so embarrassing." She brought her palms to her eyes and closed them. "I'm usually a lot more prepared."

"It can't be as embarrassing as not looking where you're going and crashing into a celebrity baker who has her arms full of cookies to deliver on Christmas Eve. Tell me, Anna. What is it you need?"

No fair. He should not have used her name like that, all caring and intimate. It set off a strange, fluttery sensation in her chest that she wasn't sure she liked or hated.

"Sugar for sure. And maybe butter," she cringed. "I didn't have time to check."

A big smile spread across his face, making the thick white beard fall away from the corner of his mouth. His bushy fake eyebrows wiggled. "Follow me."

LIGHTS FLICKED on from their motion as they walked down the corridor. As they approached a door, he took a badge on a black lanyard from inside his Santa coat. He swiped the plastic through a reader and the door, marked *Food Service & Cafeteria*, clicked open.

"You work here?" she asked.

"I do."

Earlier he had told her he was new in town. "Wait," she asked, "are you the new chef?"

He was leading them toward a shelf of dry goods but turned around to answer. "That would be me."

She had read about him in the newspaper. Orange County guy, left the area, recently returned. He pointed to a lone ten-pound bag of sugar on a middle shelf. "We only have one. Our shipment's"—she finished the sentence with him—"been delayed."

He took the bag off the shelf and instead of handing it over, he held it to his chest. "You can have this under one condition."

"And what is that?" she asked, biting her cheek to tamp her grin. She might just be able to salvage those orders, leave them on her customers' doorsteps by midnight. And, well, he was pretty cute.

"What did you do with the busted-up cookies, the ones that didn't land in the street?"

"They're on the counter at my shop."

"Then I'll make you a very special Christmas deal," he said.

"A deal?" She bit harder.

"The sugar is yours, but you have to give me the broken cookies."

"That's a deal I'm happy to make, but what are you going to do with them?"

"I have to prepare dessert for the kids tomorrow, and without the sugar I need something else to work with. Cookie crumbles will be equally sweet."

SHE GAVE him a ride to the bakery. He stood aside while she unlocked the door, disarmed the alarm, turned on the back-room lights. Once inside, he set the sugar on the counter by the mixer, and went to the coat rack outside her office.

He unbuckled his wide black Santa belt and took off the big red jacket. She tried not to look too long at his muscular arms or the curves of the chest muscles that moved under his worn-gray tee.

He unfastened the white strap that encircled his waist, the one attached to his belly padding. "Silicone," he narrated as he undressed. "Jiggles like the real thing." He patted the tee-shirt with both hands where the padding had just sat. But his real belly did not jiggle.

The soft cotton was tight around his chest, and loose over his stomach. From what she could tell so far, he was . . . What was the phrase Carli liked to use when talking about gorgeous celebs? That's right: *Cut.*

He put one hand on the counter to balance as he slipped off his big black shoes and stepped out of the baggy red pants. Just like the tee shirt, the jeans under his Santa suit fit him quite nice.

Yes, Santa was definitely cut.

He pulled off the beard and the eyebrows, set the gold glasses on the counter. Without the glare of the lenses, she could see him better now. His eyes, they still twinkled. Underneath his white wig was a tousled mop of salt and pepper hair. Tousled like a Sunday morning. Tousled like a Sunday morning of lazy, we-have-all-day-because-my-kids-are-in-New-York sex.

For example.

She cleared her throat. Maybe that would help wipe the images from her mind. Watching him undress had provided new information to process, given her a whole new idea.

"Shall we?" she asked, pointing to the counter with the sugar, although right now with him standing nearby, making cookies was the least of what she wanted to do.

Customers!

Okay, focus. They washed their hands and put hairnets on. She laid her recipes on the counter. She didn't have to tell him much; he knew just what to do.

While she made the dough, he mixed the icing, portioned it into bowls and added color. As they waited for the first sheets of cookies to bake, he leaned back against the counter. "So, tell me, Anna, why do you hate Christmas?"

There was her name again—not fair—and his question hit her from left field. She looked at him, surprised. "I don't hate Christmas."

"Okay, maybe hate is too strong. 'Dislike'? 'Averse to'? You traffic in nuts, so maybe 'allergic to'? I know it's not because you have to make a ton of cookies—it's clear you love to bake."

She shot him a sidelong smile. "I do love to bake. Not under the gun like this, but otherwise yes, I do." That was why, instead of continuing to bang her head against a wall to find a job after she and Blake split, she decided to start her own business.

"So you love to bake, but you . . . are displeased . . . with Christmas." His crooked smile and two dimples were more adorable than she cared to admit.

"I. Do. Not. Hate. Christmas." But even though she laughed as she said it, her volume had gone up—not to a yell, more like when the mixer was running and she was trying to talk to the kids—and it kind of might sound like maybe she was not so crazy about Christmas. "The thing with Christmas is . . . " She didn't usually share with strangers. But he was here, helping her fix the mess, and he had asked the question.

As she spoke, she looked at him, noticed the smudge of icing beside his nose. Without thinking, she stepped close and gently wiped it away. She wanted to lick her finger, taste the sugar from his skin, but they were baking, and that was not exactly aligned with health department regulations.

His breath caught when she touched him, or maybe it

had been hers. Regardless, some invisible barrier crumbled. His gaze remained on her, his eyes ready to listen to whatever she would say.

"I miss my kids." It wasn't any deep dark confession, just a simple truth. "They're with their father and his new wife, doing things we used to do as a family. I don't miss him; I don't want to get back together, but being without the kids at the holidays is hard."

Those eyes of his were empathetic; he hadn't needed to say "I get it" for her to tell he could relate.

"How about you? You obviously don't hate Christmas— I mean anyone who invests in the silicone padding can't hate it." She patted her own belly to illustrate as she spoke. "But playing Santa probably isn't part of your chef job description."

He hesitated. Maybe he didn't want to tell her. "I'd wanted to volunteer at the hospital for many years, but . . . I couldn't." She felt her forehead tighten, wondering why not.

"My kid got sick many years ago and we spent a December there. The people were amazing. They made the weeks we had left very meaningful. I wanted to do something in return, but I guess I needed more time."

He crossed his arms, then put his hands back where they had been, resting on the counter behind him. "But then the chef job in the kitchen opened up, and—I don't know—it seemed like a safe way to come back. I hardly saw any kids—once or twice maybe in a hallway or elevator—but just being here again and remembering the kindness was enough for me to know I had to try the Santa thing. At least once."

"I'm so sorry," she said. "I can't imagine."

Here she was complaining about missing her kids to someone whose child was not going to bang through the door in a few days after their trip, blast their music, dump their dirty laundry, roll their teenage eyes. And that little boy she saw clinging to James' shoulder earlier; it had to have rebroken his heart.

She wanted to ask him what happened, how he had been able to cope, but those weren't the kinds of things you asked a virtual stranger; she trusted he would share if he felt like opening up.

"You *can* imagine. You're a parent. It's what you feel right now, the missing. Only it cuts deeper into your soul, and it never goes away."

She was thinking it was good she hadn't maimed him, and just then the timer beeped. The numbers on the oven display had blurred, and she paused to wipe her eyes.

He helped her take the sheets out and slide them onto the cooling racks. An easy quiet settled between them. He iced and she decorated the different shapes, then placed them in the boxes.

"Hey," he started as they finished up, "can I help you drop them off?"

"You don't have to do that. I'm sure you have plans tonight." She hoped he didn't.

"I'd love to, Anna." His voice sent her insides fluttering again as they packed and loaded her car. Before leaving, they took off the hairnets; he put his Santa suit back on.

THEY MADE it a couple of hours before midnight, her relieved clients opening their doors with delight. "This is my friend Santa," she said to each one as he handed them their cookies. He apologized to the parents, explained the reason for the delay, took photos with their kids.

When the last drop-off was done, they drove through a hilltop Laguna neighborhood famous for its lights to ogle all the yards. "Do you have a favorite Christmas tradition?" he asked as they snaked down the winding road.

"Tradition? I'm not sure. That implies repetition, and the way things work out, especially with the bakery, the kids usually spend it with their dad. But a couple of years ago they were home and after the deliveries we went to Crystal Cove to see the Christmas tree. They loved that."

She could feel how smiling loosened the tension in her face. That was a fun night; she had loved it too. "So?" he asked.

"So what?"

"Why don't we go?"

They hiked past the historic cottages with retro decorations in the windows and tromped down the steps to the beach. A handful of people were just leaving; the park was about to close. For a little while, the two of them would be alone.

The tree was fully decorated and lit in golden lights, topped with a shining star. She pointed out, in the distance, the silhouette of Catalina Island.

The waves crashed and retreated, giving the sand a sugary glaze. Next year, she would design a Crystal Cove cookie, a green Christmas tree on a golden beach, blue water out behind it.

She took a photo of the tree and texted it to the kids. Three hours ahead, they would be asleep now, but they would see it Christmas morning. Then who knows what possessed her, she texted their father too. "Hi. The kids seem like they're having a wonderful time. Merry Christmas, Blake. -A."

She felt James' hand on her elbow, and he gestured to a

piece of driftwood the waves had weathered smooth. "Shall we have a seat?"

They sat, and he turned to her, his eyes twinkling for real now as they reflected the moonlight and the stars. "Still hate Christmas?" he asked, putting his arm around her shoulder to give a squeeze and draw her close.

She chuckled and shook her head. "I told you, I don't hate . . . " That grin of his. Damn. It made her want to play along. "No, James. I no longer hate Christmas."

He slapped his leg, the baggy Santa pants still on. "Yes! I'm glad to hear that. Maybe my work here is done."

He was funny, and she laughed. But then, she shook her head, feigned a face that said he was wrong. "I don't think your work is done."

"No?" He barely contained his smile.

"No." And with that she kissed him, stroked his cheek, felt his sexy stubble as she trailed her fingers along his jaw. His mouth was welcoming and eager, his exploration sweeter than she had imagined.

They paused and pressed their foreheads to one another. "So what were you planning to do tonight?" he whispered. "Before we . . . bumped into each other?" It was a cute pun and also apt—things felt familiar between them. It was as if they'd known each other a long while.

"I was going to watch a romantic comedy. Or three."

"I have an idea." He squeezed her hand and kissed it. "We could watch one together. You can pick the movie."

She outlined his lips with her fingertip, and he placed his arm around her shoulders again. "I don't want to watch a movie after all," she said, "but I would love to take you home."

HE WORE no goofy elf hat like the studly rink guy in her dream. No jingle bells pealed as he moved down her body. Just like at her bakery, she didn't have to tell him much; he knew *exactly* what to do. Their sex was spiced with laughter; it was passionate and dirty. In more ways than one, this Santa made her Christmas so much sweeter.

2

SANTA & CLARA

In the dream, she was working on her laptop, preparing a slide deck for the next training presentation. The first-class cabin lights had dimmed a couple of hours ago, and most of the passengers were sleeping. The flight attendants were on break; no one had passed by in a while.

The plane gave a gentle jounce, and then a few more, harder in quick succession. A chiming sound penetrated her earphones before they filled with the captain's voice, a nice baritone, weighted and deep.

Considerate of the sleepers, he spoke softer than at take-off. It was as if he whispered just to her. "We're going to turn on the fasten seatbelt sign—we're encountering some turbulence. Please stay in your seat."

She checked her belt out of habit, although she knew it was secure. The bumps came faster, the cabin doors rattled, bags in the overhead compartments thumped. The sudden dip of an air pocket made her stomach tumble while the aircraft banged side to side. She glanced at the overhead panel. No yellow masks dangled, which she took as a very good sign.

Something tugged on the top of her seat, and she felt a presence behind her. A man was losing his balance and, next thing, the handsome stranger fell in her lap.

"I'm so sorry," he said in his sexy voice, flashing her a smile. It was the airplane pilot, especially good-looking up this close. As he moved off her lap and into the seat beside her, she noticed the epaulets on his shoulder and the green tie with tiny Santas. His forearms were strong and muscular, his fitted white shirt was tucked into snug black pilot pants.

He lifted the armrest between them and unbuckled her seatbelt. The tongue clanked as it fell from the buckle. "Don't worry, I've got you," he said, and pulled her onto his lap.

She straddled him, felt him hard beneath her dampness. His hands traveled up her arms, setting off an electrical current, and he gently cupped her face. "I'll go back to the cockpit if this isn't okay, but we have a wonderful opportunity. The plane's equipped with autopilot; my first mate just drank more coffee." His thumb stroked her lip, and he bit his own; his rising hunger was palpable. "It's late, Clara. May I give you a good reason to stop working?"

She undid his belt and zipper; he lifted her dress above her hips, draped a light blanket around them. It was hard to tell what was turbulence or the two of them heaving and bucking. He brought her to the height of pleasure; she hadn't had this in so long. She bit his shoulder to stifle her cry, his epaulets rough against her lips. Their climax was near simultaneous, which surprised her since he was a stranger. The thought came to her that although the airlines were never easy to deal with, she really did love to fly.

HER PHONE ALARM went off at 5:30, early enough to go for a run along the creek and a swim at the international center. Then a quick shower, grab breakfast, pack, and head to the client's office. She had one training session left to facilitate this morning. There would be no afternoon class today. The project manager had asked her to wrap by noon. The office party for the few hundred employees started off with a fancy luncheon. Hard to believe it was already Christmas Eve; she had landed in San José on December first.

On the way back from her run and swim, she printed her boarding pass, a backup to the e-version on her phone. Thank you, courtesy upgrade; her assigned seat was in the first-class cabin. As she turned on the shower, she remembered the dream. That flight was pretty amazing. Although the only part that came close to real life was how much she had been working.

After twenty-plus years of consulting, she had finally landed one of the world's largest tech firms as a client, but her celibacy streak wasn't healthy; she really needed to get laid. Preferably by a handsome stranger with muscular arms and broad uniformed shoulders and . . . *Right*. With her schedule and so much travel, that was only likely to happen in one place: her fantasies. Maybe she should ask the Tooth Fairy or the Easter Bunny or, given the season, Santa.

The client's Silicon Valley campus sported a festive air. Everyone was in good spirits. Her training room had been decorated overnight—fake snow, a string of lights around the whiteboard and, standing beside her podium, a miniature Queen-Anne gingerbread house complete with a pointy turret.

By ten minutes to noon, she wrapped up, wished everyone a good celebration. As she put her laptop into her bag, the project manager poked her head in the door. "Clara, we're thrilled with the training you've done for us, and you've been working really hard. Please, join us for the party."

She had been on for three weeks solid—engaged, focused, and energetic. As soon as the high wore off, she knew what would happen: She would quickly turn depleted and exhausted. Besides, it would be good to remain a bit reserved since this was her long-sought client—great for her CV and reputation, and they had promised much more work. Better to keep up the professional facade, not get overly chummy. She wanted to end the year on a high note, get to the airport, sit quietly alone in the passenger lounge.

"That's so kind, but I'll have to decline," she said. "The traffic and the airport will be madness. I should leave plenty of time to make my flight."

The truth was, she didn't have to rush. She could stand to miss her plane because her Christmas plans were light. But that she would spend Christmas by herself was something no one here needed to know.

"We won't take no for an answer," the project manager countered. "Everyone lets their hair down; it's always so much fun. Come, have a drink with us—really, you must."

THE EVENT SPACE WAS FANTASTIC, the holiday decorations totally over the top. But what most caught her eye in the whole huge ballroom was Santa. Of course he wore the big red suit and the snow-white beard and wig, but what called to her from where she stood was his own magnetic smile. He had presence and charisma, and a strong feeling instantly overtook her: She knew him.

Someone pointed and said his name, and she realized why he seemed so familiar. It wasn't destiny or soulmates. The angels could stop singing. He was just an actor from the nineties, the star of a Christmas movie. She had seen it once, many years ago—some corny romantic flick. She couldn't remember the exact name, something about a Christmas wish.

The project manager waved Clara over and drew her into her circle. "This is Clara," she said each time a new person joined the conversation. After shaking her hand, one of them said, "It's a lovely name, and really not so common. The only other Clara I know of was Santa's wife in that old movie."

The project manager gasped and clapped her mouth. "You know, you're right!" she said, "Excuse us, we'll be right back."

She grabbed Clara's hand, marched her over, and introduced her to Santa. Up close he had eyes that sparkled, but maybe they just reflected the holiday lights. He extended his hand, and her pulse began to hammer. "Enchanted to meet you, Clara."

The project manager talked to him about the luncheon's activities. Clara heard something about a game. Then the woman grinned at Clara and politely drifted away. Santa reached into a box beside his big chair and pulled out a red and white hat. He gestured, *come here*, and put it on her. The white pom-pom flopped and brushed her ear, and then his voice followed. "Clara, with that name you'll have to help me with the crowd, play the role of my wife for a little while."

Her belly did a nervous flip and she fought the urge to

run. She knew how to handle a business crowd, but she was not a performer. And she could not remember the plot of his movie, which would make it hard to play along.

But over the past three weeks, she had met most of the people in this room, and they were a friendly, laid-back bunch. She didn't need to fear this. Besides, it could actually be good for business, help strengthen client rapport. She stood taller and shifted her stance, took on her power pose. She would stand up here and play his wife—that is, until she could sneak away to catch her flight.

Santa reached for Clara's hand, and together they stepped to the mic. She tried to ignore the warmth of his skin while he joshed the crowd and explained the next activity.

"The elves are bringing around paper and pens. Write down your Christmas wish so Santa knows what it is. And if you want a chance to win the company raffle, make sure to put your name on it. The elves will collect them, and the lucky winners get a prize."

She didn't know what came over her, but she turned to him and spoke. "Santa, honey, can I have the mic?"

He looked at her, his smile bright but also a tad unsure. "Why of course my darling Clara, anything you wish."

He handed her the microphone and she brought it to her lips. "I think Santa should write down his Christmas wish too, don't you all agree?" She looked at him out of the corner of her eye and caught his glowing smile. The guests clapped and cheered in agreement. Since there was no elf with paper nearby, she took her green pen and a sticky note from this morning's class out of her dress pocket.

He shifted his pursed lips left and right, pretending to think about it hard. He wrote something down and folded the paper over. An elf came by, and Santa dropped his wish into the hat.

Then he took the mic back from her, "Now your wish, too, my dear Clara." Handing her a piece of paper, he said, "Write the first thing that comes to mind." Then he turned his attention back to amusing the crowd, and she didn't bother doing it.

She moved aside to let him do his Santa shtick, took a seat at the nearest table. He was funny and cute and jolly; often he threw back his head and laughed. It was delightful to watch him have a good time and to see how the large group responded.

When lunch was served, he took a break, stopped by her seat to pick her up. They walked to the bar for a glass of wine with his hand at the small of her back. The feeling made her regret her choice. *Maybe I* should *have made a wish.*

When they returned to his spot with the Santa chair, he glanced at his watch and out at the crowd. Silverware still clinked as people ate, and voices remained animated. The guests weren't ready just yet for him to begin again.

He stood facing Clara and took her hands, said he had a question. "Did you write down your wish?"

She laughed at his perception and sheepishly told him she hadn't. From inside his red Santa coat, he took out a pen and a slip of paper. "Write it down, and put it in the hat—do it for real this time."

She wished she hadn't had that erotic dream last night, some lingering effect of it still with her. It wasn't typically her nature to share such personal information, but something in his voice coaxed it from her; she liked how he took charge. Plus, she would never see him again, and so she had nothing to lose. She wrote the truth: *A sexy tryst on a plane with a man like this Santa.*

He watched her write, but he was too far away to read her purposely tiny script. And sorry, Santa, there was no way—she was not writing her name.

AS SHE WAITED for her taxi to the airport, she wondered if she should have found him and said a proper goodbye. It felt like there was some real attraction between them. But she reminded herself he was playing a part; he had been hired by the corporation. From his Santa costume and his wish-filled hat to how he looked at her and seemed flirty—it wasn't actual chemistry, it just felt that way because he was an actor.

The flight attendant offered her a drink and lowered the tray table next to her, the one for the aisle seat. With so many passengers distracted with holiday plans, hauling their gifts and overweight luggage, that would be a real wish come true—no chatty, annoying neighbor boxing her in on the flight home.

She looked out the plane's window, pre-takeoff activity buzzing around her—the zzhht of the wing flaps, the call button chimes, shuffling bags to fit in the cabin bins. The clink of ice falling into buckets, a sputter of steam, the scent of coffee brewing.

The sun was about to set, streaking the sky with pastel colors. The clouds were thin and wispy; it should be a good night to fly. And then she thought of Santa and wondered what he was doing. Maybe he lived in L.A. like her, but with Christmas he would most likely jet off to Tahoe or Park City.

Something grazed her arm, and her disappointment grew. She couldn't bring herself to look. Please, not someone sitting next to her, but alas the seatbelt clicked. "Oops, sorry," said a voice she knew and only then did she turn to see.

Out of context and without the costume, he looked different but no less magnetic. There was a whooshing in her ears and a thudding in her chest. His sparkling eyes went wide—he seemed incredulous and . . . maybe nervous? "Hello, Clara. Wow," he shook his head, "I can't believe it's you."

He was breathless like he had been running, like he got to the airport late. She was about to ask about the rest of the party but the captain's voice broke in. "Folks . . . from the flight deck . . . We're all anxious to get to our destinations, but we're going to be on the tarmac for a while—I'm afraid we're in for some delay."

SANTA AND CLARA bumped elbows awkwardly countless times, and he lifted the armrest between them. The flight attendants plied the impatient crowd with snacks and soft drinks. And then someone whined that the wi-fi died and soon the passengers were ready to mutiny.

"I think this is a job for Santa," he said to her, getting up to speak to the flight attendant.

When he returned to their row, he retrieved his bag and took out the scrunched-up costume. He put it on right then and there, over his everyday clothes. As he buckled up his Santa belt, he looked at her with a raised brow. "What do you say, Clara—do you still have your hat?"

She took it out of her bag and put it on while the flight

attendant made an announcement. "Ladies and gentlemen, we're in for a special treat this Christmas Eve. Guess who just happens to be a passenger on our flight."

They did their routine from the party, and the flight attendants played the elves. Only this time he didn't press her to write her wish, and mostly he avoided her eyes. Her racing heart slowed to its usual pace, and she forced a holiday smile.

After they'd gone through the cabin, the passengers gave a round of cheery applause, and someone clinked a glass with a spoon. Right, now she remembered, the final scene from his movie was—what else?—a magical, romantic kiss.

He took her hand and pulled her close, and brought his lips toward hers. Their kiss was brief and chaste, and the crowd wouldn't have it; the passengers continued to cheer and tink.

By now the two of them were laughing, and their next attempt was far less modest. But the passengers were a harsh reminder: The way his mouth felt against hers, the sizzling connection between them, it only meant he was an exceptional actor.

Soon, everyone quieted down once the wi-fi came back online, and the flight attendants thanked the two of them profusely. Instead of returning to their seats, Santa gently took her hand and led her through an unmarked door beside the galley. "Crew rest area," he said with a sheepish grin once they were inside. The space was tight, with a narrow bunk, the mattress neatly made with white sheets. With him still holding her hand, there was hardly enough air to breathe.

It took her a second to realize. "Oh, my goodness," she said, "You read my paper, my thing." Her cheeks blazed like two burning coals; she couldn't bring herself to say *wish*.

"Clara, don't be embarrassed." He stroked her cheek where she was flushed. "Don't be embarrassed with me. Please?"

She took a deep breath to try to think. Did it really matter that he was an actor? Her dream had left her with an unquenched desire, and she had made a sexy wish, one with which he seemed happy to comply. So she nodded okay, and soon they were kissing again, and it was not at all chaste or just once.

"How did you do this?" she asked while his kisses blanketed her neck.

"I asked the lead flight attendant for a quiet corner where we could have a moment alone. She gave me a knowing look and said she had the perfect place. But are you okay with this? If not, we can go back to our seats. We can watch out the window and see our luggage get tossed and dented while we wait to take off."

She laughed and looked up into those eyes, put her arms around his neck. "I think this is definitely the better option."

On the door behind them, he slid the lock to occupied. "So then, tell me about this fantasy, Clara—what did you have in mind? Or, wait, why don't you show me?"

She helped him take off his Santa costume and then his everyday clothes and pointed to the small bed. His flash of shyness was the sweetest thing as he pulled her onto his lap. More kissing and then she straddled him, felt him hard beneath her dampness. His hands traveled up her arms, setting off an electrical current. His thumb stroked her lip, his rising hunger palpable.

He lifted her dress above her hips and draped a light blanket around them. There wasn't any turbulence, just the two of them heaving and bucking. Then somewhere in the background, the captain's voice emerged sounding muffled: ". . . cleared for takeoff. In 90 minutes, we'll be in L.A."

"I'm almost there," she gasped, her nails digging into Santa's back. He moaned her name and came with her, his shoulder stifling her cry.

As the plane took flight, he held her tight against him. They looked out at the city below: their client's green campus, the football stadium, the squiggly track of the amusement park's roller coaster, the aquamarine pools of the swimming center.

They got dressed and left the cabin, discreetly one at a time. Back in their seats, he turned to her. "Clara, I have a question."

She thought she had dodged it, but apparently she hadn't. "What are you doing tomorrow?" he asked, "How are you spending Christmas?"

She nudged his knee playfully. "Sorry, but that's two."

"Pick one," he said, his teasing smile dimming. She wanted to answer neither.

But she did, and it was the truth. "I don't have any plans." She paused and waited for his shocked reaction, but all he did was take her hand. Expectation filled the air while he waited for her to say more.

"Everyone I would want to spend Christmas with already had plans to go visit family or in-laws or on vacation. Don't get me wrong, I would be welcome to tag along, but I didn't want to be the pity invitation. I'm fine flying solo on the holiday, especially after working so much, but no one ever believes me. I don't want to agree to plans just for the sake of not being alone."

"I agree, solitude is wonderful, but, please, join me and my daughter. At least come for dinner. Or dessert, or a drink. Whatever makes you comfortable." She started to speak, but he touched his finger to her lips. "I'm not asking out of pity."

"It's a wonderful invitation, and you just fulfilled my fantasy-wish." She put her hand on his wrist. "But you're an actor," she said, as much to herself as to him, "playing a role; you were Santa giving a present."

"Let me show you something." He reached into his pocket and unfolded a scrap of paper. "Remember, you asked me to write my wish too?" She took it from his hand and read his words, in green ink from the pen she'd loaned him.

To see Clara again.

And now she remembered another beat from his movie. Right before the big finale—that kiss—it turned out he and Clara had both separately made the same Christmas wish.

"Clara, I do the Santa thing every year, and I always write something bogus in case others happen to see it. This time I wrote from the heart since fake wishes can't come true."

"How did you know which was mine?" she wanted to know.

"You were the only one who didn't write your name."

He used his finger to lift her chin while he held her gaze intently. "If you'd rather not see me on Christmas, I certainly understand. But as Santa and Clara we already know we're compatible, and we just had amazing sex. So could we make a date for another day because, Clara, I still truly wish to see you again."

3

SANTA CRU

In the dream, they rode the old Ferris wheel at the boardwalk amusement park. Tucked into a seat that rocked in the breeze, they looked out at the Pacific, stretched before them like a painted sunset canvas. The motion intensified as they started to kiss, Sofia and her beau. It was lush and rich, a kiss like her vineyard's old-vine Zinfandel.

As the stars came out, they reclined in the seat, which was now somehow more like a bed. They undressed each other like teenagers, removing only the essential items. He rolled on top, she told him she wanted him, and with a passionate moan he complied.

Time stood still as the Ferris wheel turned, their quasi-hammock swaying high above the coast. The two of them intimately connected, she gazed into his blue eyes. Her climax crested at the high point of their orbit, in the arms of the man she loved. This—what they were doing up so high and letting herself fall for him—they were two of the boldest things she had ever done.

They cuddled together. He ran his fingers through her

dark hair. Their bed, their seat, slowed back to its gentle lilt. The Ferris wheel revolved; their bench continued to descend. As they got three-quarters around, he turned to her and suddenly said, "That was incredible, and I love you, but I can't do this anymore."

It took her a moment to process his words, and she felt her face scrunch in confusion. While she sputtered her half-baked questions, he reached behind them and pulled a lever. Their seat tipped sharply forward although somehow he remained on the ride. She on the other hand slid straight off and whistled through the air. Until she landed like a weighted beach ball, *whump* in the sand.

SHE RAN around the winery preparing for tomorrow's Christmas Eve bash, the annual release of the limited harvest holiday wine, Santa Cru, that perfectly captured the vineyard's cool winter terroir. As in previous years, she had hired a jazz ensemble, and there would be a strolling dinner and drinks. Colorful ceramic trays of *petiscos*, Portuguese appetizers, on every available surface: miniature *bifana* sandwiches, caramelized figs and goat cheese, savory salt cod fritters.

Imagining the wonderful smells of the food helped ease the bitter finish of her dream. He had dumped her, one year ago to the day, December twenty-third. They had met twelve months earlier, when she had noticed a vine that looked sick. If you didn't act fast, a season's crop could go bust, so she had immediately called a viti-culturist.

He came out to the vineyard from the local college's agriculture extension, and she showed him the unhealthy vine. When the back of their hands accidentally touched, their attraction bloomed, instantaneous and intense.

For their first date, he picked her up at the winery's tasting room on the river in Capitola, and they went to the boardwalk amusement park. Their last ride that night was the chairlift that glided high above the coast—old fashioned, mellow, and slow. They held hands and kissed, both excited, she thought, to see a relationship grow.

From their first meeting she had felt right at home with him, although she wasn't in any hurry. There was value in waiting, she knew; you didn't run a vineyard, the cellar full of aging wine and expect overnight miracles to occur.

Their real breakup was only slightly less sudden than the dumping in her dream, and she reminded herself yet again, it was probably for the best. For one thing, their Christmas traditions did not align. She would always have the winery front and center this time of year, while every Christmas Eve, in a longstanding tradition, he dutifully traveled to be with his parents.

She took a deep breath, squared her shoulders, and shook off the memory. Before the breakup, Christmas had been her favorite time of year. It would be again, she was sure, but it might take a little more time. The hurt and the rejection, the shock of his change of heart—it had faded some but it still smarted.

But she couldn't afford to be a grinch when it came to holiday cheer. Tomorrow night, she would need to put on a smile and play the good hostess. The media would be coming, food and wine writers and aficionados, the bloggers and the influencers, photographers and videographers galore. They would help her keep wine sales high and, well into the new year, the vineyard's social media humming.

As for her romantic disenchantment, well, there simply was no room on Christmas Eve for anything tart or sour.

The winery's small staff helped her finish the decorations. Cottony snow batting woven among the candle lights on the wrought-iron chandelier, holly over the stone fireplaces, cedar boughs and roping with golden lights draped above the terrace archways, playful ornaments hung behind the tasting bar.

She took photos with her phone and texted them to her parents. They had—finally—left the Santa Cruz Mountains to spend Christmas in the Douro Valley. Gratitude filled her heart as she pictured them on a sunny terrace. The two of them had worked so hard for so long, she was happy they had listened when she encouraged them to go.

In her office, she sat at her desk, called everyone to confirm—the caterers, the scheduled staff, temporary servers and the valets, the all-important Santa sent by a local talent agency. She listened as his phone rang a few times, then went to voicemail. While she waited to leave a message, she thought, "Hmm, he has a nice voice."

CHRISTMAS EVE DAY, she checked off the final preparations. It was important to get tonight right. Guests loved this event; it was cozy and elegant, and they bought lots of wine.

In the late afternoon, she went down to the underground cave to check on the decorations there, since guests loved to tour the cellar. Her parents had built it into the sandstone, a wide circular tunnel lined with racks to hold all the barrels. It was cool and dry and softly lit. The smell of earth and oak reminded her why she had wanted to be a vintner and take over when her parents retired.

She worked with the cellar hand to hang more strings of tiny lights—on the barrels, over the archways, in the tasting room from the chandelier—until the cave gave off a dreamy glow.

Back upstairs, she did one last walk-through. Everything looked how she had envisioned—warm and inviting, luxurious and rustic. And, although she might not fully feel it herself, merry and festive and bright.

And then it was time to change into her party clothes, a floor-length velvet dress the color of a rich merlot and glossy black strappy sandals. As she checked her hair in the mirror in her office, her phone buzzed with a missed call alert.

She listened to the voicemail and had to remind herself to breathe. Santa's voice was muffled and stuffy, foggy and contrite. "I'm so sorry for the last-minute call but I've come down with some kind of bug. I won't be able to make it tonight, but it's going to be okay; I have a colleague who agreed to fill in. I've briefed him on your party plans, and he's memorized the script. He'll be there early, and—"

Jesus H. *Seriously?* Santa was cancelling *now?*

"Really, there's no need to worry," her old Santa continued in his nasal tone, "He knows how to play the part. Plus he's a great guy—charming but unassuming, and he knows a ton about wine."

AS PROMISED, New Santa arrived early for the gig, already dressed in full Claus regalia. It wasn't only his rotund stature and red suit, or the white gloves and beard and wig—no, that was hardly the end of it. He must have spent some serious time in an artist's makeup chair. His bulbous nose was red at the tip, with two rosy cheeks and deep old Santa wrinkles across his forehead. His eyes behind the round spectacles were a pleasant green, and jolly laugh lines crinkled kindly at the corners.

From the moment he arrived he spoke in a deep Santa Claus voice. He ho-ho-ho-ed at all the right times, and he didn't break character the rest of the night.

Old Santa had been right—the new guy had memorized the evening's agenda, stuck closely to her script. He knew all the little anecdotes she had written about each wine, including the evening's centerpiece, her flagship Santa Cru. He even remembered to include the bit about those particular vines and their fruit needing extra TLC.

She didn't remember telling Old Santa about that, but it had been a while since they had spoken; the season had been so busy, she must have just forgotten.

As the night went on and the music played and the guests laughed and ate and drank, she couldn't help but observe New Santa from afar. His upbeat presence, the way he charmed the guests—she realized that at some point in the evening her mood had turned surprisingly light. If he were wine, she mused as she watched him, he would be smooth and plummy, low in tannins and acidity.

He really was the perfect man for the job. Sorry Old Santa, but she would get this one's number, book him for next year before the end of the night.

AS THE GUESTS were getting ready to leave, the staff took their places by the wooden door. They had a table full of gift bags to pass out, filled with wine-themed holiday treats. She would help distribute them in a minute, but first she went to talk to New Santa and pay him so he could leave.

"The pleasure was all mine," he said in that jolly Santa voice as he started toward the door. "And I'll stay a bit longer to help with the gifts if you don't mind—that's Santa's job, after all."

One time as they both reached for the same bag to give to a departing guest, her hand bumped New Santa's white glove, and it sent a shiver straight down her spine. But it wasn't the kind of shiver that came from cool evening air. If she hadn't still been so wary after the breakup, she might ask him to stay for a drink.

He wished each guest a merry Christmas, and ho-ho-ho-ed until the last one left, maintaining the festive air.

While her staff began to clean up, he turned to her and in his rich Santa voice he asked, "Are you happy with how the evening went?"

"I am," she said, "and I'd like to hire you for next year—I hope it's early enough that your calendar isn't booked."

"That can probably be arranged," he said with a nervous smile, "but Sofia, first there's something I have to say."

He began to take off his Santa outfit—the red jacket, the red pants, the belly padding, the white gloves. His fingers, his hands, they looked familiar; for some reason they made her chest ache. Then quickly he pulled off the beard and the glasses, lifted a molded mask of wrinkled skin, took out his green contact lenses. And now—she inhaled a sharp breath—it was all too clear who he really was.

"What the . . ." Her voice dropped into silence as he started to explain. "The guy you booked happens to work in my office. A few weeks ago he mentioned the talent agency he moonlights for had hired him to play Santa at your winery. Then this afternoon, I saw him leaving work, looking extremely under the weather. It was obvious he wasn't in any shape to play Santa, and I asked what he planned to do. He felt terribly bad but said he had no choice but to cancel. I know how important Christmas Eve is to you, so I told him I knew the winery and could fill in."

"But it's Christmas Eve—what about your family tradition, your visit to your parents?"

"I couldn't go knowing you would be in a bind tonight."

Anger squeezed her chest, like a wine press crushing her ribs. "Is this your penance, your . . . your way of easing a guilty conscience? It was a year ago! We have no more ties."

He dropped his wig and reached for her hands, but she yanked them hard away. "That's not what it is. I pictured how upset you'd be when he told you he wouldn't make it, and . . . the thought of that . . . I couldn't stand it."

Her eyes widened and she sniggered at what he said. "What about how upset I'd be when you ended things—ended *us*—out of the blue like that? How come *that* didn't seem to bother you?"

"Sofia, of course it bothered me—and that's an understatement. I tried to call and text you several times, but you never ans—"

"No, you're right—I didn't answer. I had been sure you felt the same way I did, and the shock of how you let me know that wasn't true was . . ." She hated thinking about that night. "I felt so stupid, and embarrassed and ashamed."

"How I treated you was inexcusable. I'm the one who owns the shame. I acted like a revolting jerk, lower than . . . powdery mildew." There was that crooked smile again, unhindered by the disguise, the smile that used to make her heart feel spacious and toasty warm.

"That's right, lower than . . . Petri disease." She couldn't help but laugh right then at their corny exchange and she noticed he instantly relaxed. When he reached for her hand again, she didn't pull it away.

"Sofia, I can't apologize enough for how deeply I hurt you and it's selfish of me to ask, but would you indulge me one more time, come with me somewhere special so we can talk?"

SHE SHOULD SAY NO, but she did not; she was strong enough that she could listen to what he had to say. Besides, learning what had happened from his perspective might give her closure; maybe it would help. Although sadness didn't have a schedule, tonight something inside her heart had begun to change; she started to feel ready to move on.

He asked if he could blindfold her once they got into the car, and reluctantly she agreed. He drove them down the mountain, along the winding road she knew. But then he made a few turns, stopped and put the car in reverse, and with the headphones he also put on her, she lost her sense of direction.

When they finally stopped and got out, the saltwater scent in the air was unmistakable. The heat of his body beside her was achingly familiar as he led her and then abruptly stopped. "Get ready," he said, although she wasn't sure what he meant.

He removed the blindfold and lifted the headphones off, wrapped her cashmere cape tighter around her. He had brought her to the boardwalk amusement park, dark except for the lights on one particular ride. A lone employee operated the controls.

"Here it comes," New Santa said, looking over his shoulder just as the sky ride chair came around the bend to scoop them up.

"Why?" was all she asked as they sat side by side. They were the only ones in the park as the seat bounced and lifted them high above the beach. When their thighs touched, she inched away. Resting against him again was a painful reminder, especially since the ride would be over in a few minutes.

"Every day since that awful night last year, I've regretted what I did. It's so cliche, I'm embarrassed to say, but I had fallen hard for you and got scared. I felt immature and not worthy of you, and I didn't know how to talk about it. It felt like something I had to solve on my own. At the time ending things seemed like the only option."

If this was closure, it was anticlimactic, and it didn't ease her year of hurt. "What am I supposed to do with that?" she asked. "And why are you telling me now?"

He took her hand and with his other he touched her face, brushed her cheek with the warm skin of his thumb. "Sofia, if it were entirely up to me, I wish we could try again."

She wasn't the type of person to cry easily, but a tear left her eye and slid down her face and soon several more followed suit. "*I* didn't make a mistake the first time. *I* wasn't the one who walked away. How can I know you won't do it again?"

Maybe she had felt ready to move on earlier, but she had never imagined it with him.

"I know, I know," he whispered as he caught a tear with his thumb. The others he intercepted gently with his lips, one by one.

He put his arm around her shoulders. After the tender

way he kissed away the tears, she let him pull her closer against him.

"I can't change the past," he said, "but I've done the work, and I can control what I do now. And I promise you with all my heart, I will never, ever do anything like that to you again."

"I don't know," she said. "I hadn't expected this, I need to give it some thought."

His expression registered disappointment but not surprise, and she turned away, looked out at the stars that glinted in the indigo sky.

"I understand," he said, and let go of her hand, moved his arm off of her shoulder. But she didn't move away. Suddenly, she wanted more of a taste of what it could feel like to be with him again.

They were quiet then, the two of them, their chair lilting with the salty breeze.

She was the one who broke the silence. Maybe she shouldn't tell him this, but what the hell, why not? "I had a dream about us last night." She looked him directly in the eye. "A dream-dream."

"Oh?" he asked, his face brightening with his familiar playful smile, the one she had missed so much.

She nodded and leaned her head against his arm, and she felt him heave a heavy sigh. "Sofia, I'm so incredibly sorry."

He took hold of her face lovingly and looked into her eyes. "I know I have a lot to do to regain your trust, but there's no denying the strength of our spark."

She leaned closer, and he met her lips with a perfect kiss, opulent and refined. And then the ride's mechanical hum ceased, and their chair slowed to a halt halfway across the park. "Oh, no!" she exclaimed, "What the . . . Are we stuck?"

With his fingertip he traced the top her cape and, underneath it, the neckline of her dress. He looked hungrily at her lips. "No, we're not stuck; I arranged for us to be alone up here so we could talk. Now tell me, Sofia," he said saucily, "what happened in your dream?"

She told him about the old Ferris wheel, their tryst, her climax in the sky. He moved one of his hands to her thigh, and with the other he gathered her dress, lifting it until he could reach under the hem.

Time stood still as she opened to him, suspended in mid-air. This—up here, taking a second chance with him—it may have been the boldest thing she had ever done.

4

SANTA & MONICA

In the dream, she sprang and dove headfirst into the sapphire pool, the surface glittering just like in the rental house photos online. The same slate stones, the same double chaise lounges, the same sun umbrellas around it. From under the water, she could hear muffled sounds as a crowd gathered on the pool deck cheering and clapping. As she swam deeper, the pressure cradled her ears, the water stroked her skin. The tiny bubbles she stirred up as she glided low in the pool tickled her body like sparkling wine on her tongue.

When she rose up out of the water, the crowd snapped into silence. As suddenly and uniformly as if a neon TV-studio sign had flashed the opposite of *Applause*, every single person flinched and turned away.

Then something splashed behind her, sending up a spray of cold water, and she turned to see what caused it. She stared as a dashing man rose from the depths like some heroic merman, and the sight of him made her instantly warm.

He was amply human below the waist although she

tried not to look, and as he moved closer he asked if he could kiss her. Setting aside her surprise, she agreed.

His soft lips tasted like saltwater, and she felt her eyes drift closed. When she opened them again, the crowd was gone. The two of them now floated alone toward a fairytale private grotto—foggy and moist, a trickling waterfall, soft cushions of moss on the boulders around them.

It was otherworldly and, better yet, perfect for having sex. Which they did—twice, she was happy to note. The first time took away the devastation of the crowd's reaction to her scars; the second time was pure untainted pleasure.

"I've never seen anyone more beautiful," her merman said, but she shook her head, *yeah, right*. Because although she desperately wanted to feel that way again, she didn't, at least not yet.

***

MONICA DOUBLE-CHECKED the house number on the stone pillar and leaned out of the convertible to press in the code. With an electronic whir, the gate began to open. While she waited, she tapped her phone to pause the music, her friends' shared *Loss Girls No More* playlist, and took in her surroundings. The winding drive, the landscaping, holy cow. Tall palms and thick, squat aloe tendrils, huge pots bursting with blossoms—a fragrant amuse-bouche at every turn. If this was how the driveway looked, she couldn't wait to see the house. And especially—a mix of nervousness and anticipation mingled inside her—its gorgeous saltwater pool.

The caretaker met her as she got out of the car and brought her inside for a tour and demo to operate the lights, the shades, the alarm. She tried to pay attention and not gape. Floor-to-ceiling windows made it feel like you could bask in the sun without walking out the door, while the wide beach, the ocean beyond, and that pool—shimmering just like in the photos and her dream—actually felt like part of the house.

The living room where she and the caretaker stood opened to the sky-lit roof. At the edge of the space, a modern, floating stairway rose to an open gallery and bedroom suites on the floor above.

The online ad and drool-worthy photos had made the place look totally over the top and from what she could see now that was true. That's why the five of them had chosen it —a splurge, a few days of luxury for close friends and, for Monica, the pool.

Once the caretaker left, she unloaded her overfull car. Six trips to carry in her roller bag and the groceries she bought on the way from Altadena. She checked her phone; it was almost noon—four hours until she would pick up her friends. They were coming from New York City, D.C., Detroit, and Chicago, probably right now meeting up at O'hare. One more leg to their trip and she would be there to greet them at LAX.

The house and the sunny terraces pulled like a magnet, begging to be explored, but that would have to wait. If she started now and worked efficiently, she could prepare their whole Christmas Eve dinner. Her friends had emailed her their favorite holiday recipe, and she was the designated cook. The arrangement made sense they all agreed, since she was the resident foodie, the serious home chef, and also had by far the shortest commute.

If it were possible anywhere to finish cooking before she had to go get them, it would be here. The catering kitchen off the everyday kitchen was outfitted for an entire staff—a wall of four ovens, a 10-burner gas range, three extra-large fridges and freezers, of course another reserved only for wine. Two dishwashers, two large sinks, on the stainless-steel counters sat mixers and blenders in multiple sizes. Shelves of pots and pans and baking sheets, dishes and bowls for a crowd, glasses for every conceivable drink.

Incredible. She shook her head. *Who actually lived like this?*

She pinned up her curls, put in her earbuds, and got ready to start working. While the ingredients for bread dough were spinning in the mixer's bowl, she took the cleaver from her portable knife case and began to chop the vegetables. She and her friends had rented vacation homes before, and she had learned not to count on finding a good set of sharp knives. Standing at the counter, she could see into the dining and living room and, outside, even more of a panoramic view—the wide strand of beach and the ocean, the Pier, and Santa Monica Mountains.

Then suddenly the air felt strange, and she had the feeling of being watched. She looked up just as she heard a man's voice say, "Don't be scared." *Yeah, right.* One hand flew to her chest; the other squeezed tighter around the cleaver. It didn't matter that he looked like a model for some Gen X magazine, or maybe a country singer; he was a stranger who had gotten into the house, and she was here alone.

She tried to remember what the caretaker said about the alarm and the panic button, although her mind had gone mostly blank. But wait, he looked vaguely familiar—he had the same friendly smile and the same aviator sunglasses as the guy in the rental website profile photo.

"I'm Luke," he said, slowly raising his hands in surrender, "the owner. And I take it you're Monica from Altadena.

Who didn't bring a pet, who doesn't smoke—and who is currently holding a cleaver."

"That's me," she said, realizing he was in part teasing, "but what are you doing here?"

"I called and texted you, but I didn't get an answer. I was at the airport, supposed to fly out of L.A. today, but there's some huge snow storm and air traffic everywhere is basically—excuse me—fucked."

She liked his demeanor, including how he looked both sheepish and bad-boy when he cursed. She pictured him taking off a cowboy hat, holding it over his heart, and saying something—anything—in that lusciously deep voice. There it was again as he said, "Your reservation was for a party of five but if your companions are flying today, I'm sorry to forecast bad news. You might want to check your phone."

THE GORGEOUS GUY with the incredible kitchen was talking and again she had to remind herself not to stare. Only this time it wasn't the house or the ocean, it was him. His tall, defined body, his cinnamon-sugar hair, his tired but gentle and very attractive face. ". . . so is it alright if I stay?"

"I'm sorry, what did you say?"

"Would it be okay if I spent the night? With all the flight cancellations, there's no hotel room around. I can stay in the pool house, where I usually live"—he pointed outside —"I'll be totally out of your way. You can keep the panic button with you, although with that knife in your hand, maybe I should be the one to have it."

She didn't need to force a smile, one formed all on its own. The way his eyebrows rose as he teased and grinned made her legs feel wobbly. It reminded her of when she used to get out of the community pool after a long swim, when it took a second to regain her balance.

"It's your house," she said, "and it's big enough for six."

He looked at her with concern as slowly she processed what this all meant. "Or certainly two," she corrected.

"We won't even bump into each other, I promise. And I'll text you when I leave—tomorrow, I assume—so you know I'm gone. And hopefully your friends will be here by then."

She told him it was no problem and started to get back to her chopping. "Thanks a lot," he said, "and nice meeting you, Monica."

"Nice meeting you, Luke. Oh, and Merry Christmas."

He winced more than he smiled, "Yeah, same to you." He turned to leave the kitchen but looked back as though he had a second thought. "Hey, I'm going to run out for something to eat—do you need anything before the stores close?"

Only now was the full impact of their short conversation fully clicking into place. Her friends would not be here this afternoon or for the big dinner she was preparing for tonight. She gestured at the canvas tote bags on the counter and the fridge full of the items she had already unpacked. "I have a ton of food, so feel free, help yourself."

"That's nice of you, thanks. I'll just take a couple of things. But first, I need a swim—this messed up day started at four a.m., and I need some exercise to clear my head." He started to walk away but then turned back. "I'm sorry. Apparently I've lost my manners. Would you care to join me?"

She ached to go in that water, to feel the buoyancy, the weightlessness. "Oh, no thanks." She pointed to the oven and the stove. "I should watch the timer, make sure nothing boils over."

What she actually ended up watching was him through the glass walls of the house. He emerged from the pool house in nothing but swim trunks and a towel in his hand. When he dove into the smoky sapphire pool, the glittering surface broke as he pierced it. Water flowed around him, his strong body whole and unaltered.

Stop.

In the past, she would have said yes and joined him, and not only to be in the water. She was single, and her sex drive was returning. But dreams and fantasies were one thing; in real life, she definitely was not ready for *that*.

What she was ready for was to hang with her friends, to laugh and feel unshakably supported. To dive into that glistening pool and swim with them, to climb out and see them happy for her, happy she was through the storm. They would no doubt cheer and clap, dance and clink glasses in a toast. They would hug her and rub her back and, although she deliberately hadn't brought a swimsuit, they would not avert their eyes.

With a deep breath, she put her ear buds back in and returned to work, intent on her cooking. The food would keep, and she would feed them once they arrived tomorrow.

After a while, something moved, she noticed from the corner of her eye. When she looked up, Luke stood in the doorway, a towel tied at his hips, unfortunately with his tee shirt back on.

That smile of his was something else, with eyes that matched in authenticity, but a touch of sadness floated behind them. She had seen that heaviness a lot this year, people going through daily life with excruciating burdens they didn't share.

"I came back to get that food—" he pointed to a brown bag of apples on the metal counter. "A couple of those would be great, but I was waiting for you to look up—I didn't want to scare you again." He looked around the kitchen and back at her. "You seem like you know what you're doing in here."

"Mostly, yes. I love to cook, and I'm the designated chef for our girl's vacation—our delayed girl's vacation," she added. He nodded sympathetically and it hit her, why not ask him? "My friends and I had planned a nice meal with a lot of food, I mean really, there's plenty. Would you like to have dinner with me later?"

THEY ATE an early meal on the terrace off the living room, overlooking the pool, the beach, and the ocean. Seated across from each other at the table with chairs for twelve, they must look like two elves at a giant's castle.

The ocean breeze blew salted air, laced with distant sounds from the pier. They ate and talked, and although they didn't know much about one another, it was pleasant and comfortable, not at all forced.

"So," he asked between bites, "Is this an annual Christmas tradition, you meeting up with your friends?"

"Actually no, but this year has been . . . special."

"Oh? In what way?" She could tell by his smile, he assumed they were celebrating. Which in a way they were, but also still grieving too. The trip was their way to visit and to put a bookend on their year of loss.

"Let's just say it's not been the best year. Mitra's mother passed away; Anya's husband announced his mistress was pregnant and he wanted a divorce; Natalie's wife said she had fallen out of love with her and also wanted to split; and

Keisha had to close her business—it was this brilliant tech startup, but a big-name investor—"

He cut in before she could finish.

"And you?" he asked, his hazel eyes intent, the question so direct she wasn't sure how to duck it. Everyone close to her knew, so she hadn't had to talk about it in a while.

"I needed surgery." Maybe that would satisfy his curiosity. Not that she needed to satisfy him—she could say whatever she wanted—but he seemed real and kind and like he actually gave a shit. Besides, she reminded herself, this wasn't a date; she had no investment in his opinion.

He kept his thoughtful gaze on her, prompting her to share. "I had a mastectomy."

"I'm sorry," he said, his voice serious and soft. "For all of you. Those are some major life rolls."

Okay, so far he wasn't reacting like she was a freak. She had gone on one blind date in the past year, and when she told the guy he had said, "Wow, that's a lot."

She had taken his words as empathy. "Yeah," she had replied, "but it's okay. I'm going to be fine, and for that I feel really, really lucky and grate—"

Her words had caught in her throat when she realized the guy had signaled for the check and put cash in the folio. "It's on me," he said as he pushed back his chair, "enjoy your lunch, but I have to go."

"Tell me about you," she said to Luke, relieved to be back in real time, "Where were you planning to go?"

"To Minneapolis." Now she was the one who waited for more when he paused. "To see my ex-sister-in-law and my niece and nephew."

"Sister-in-law as in ex-wife's sister, or brother's or sister's . . .?"

"My brother's ex-wife."

"That's nice—you must be on good terms. A lot of families..."

His face did a funny thing then, like it was changing shape, contorting to hold back emotion. "He died earlier this year. In an accident. He was just shy of turning fifty, a successful auto racing driver."

"Oh, Luke, I am so sorry."

"Thanks," he said, putting down his fork. "Been a hard time, for all of us, but it's been hardest on the kids."

This would be their first Christmas without him. She wanted to reach across the table and touch his hand, but she stopped. They might be sharing the place for a night, but they didn't know each other.

"Hey. I have a proposal," he said, his voice and face brightening a sliver. "It's Christmas Eve; you've made a wonderful meal—thank you for that, by the way; so much better than apples—and neither of us seems like a serial killer. What do you say we try to make it a fun holiday evening?"

She felt the smile in her cheeks at his dry humor. "I say it's a wonderful idea. But just in case, remember, I have my knives."

His laugh loosened something tight and tense inside her and whatever it was spread warmth throughout her body. "So, what shall we do, for fun?"

"I realize I'm no substitute for your friends, but what would you do if they were here?"

She looked around, inhaled the sea air. "I'm sure we would take a walk on the beach and go to the pier to watch the sunset. Then we would probably sit outside in your nice chaise lounges with herbal tea, or wine—" She pictured the five of them sitting out here together, with their banter and jokes and laughter, "—yes, we would drink a lot of wine—and talk until we couldn't keep our eyes open." She didn't mention her plan for the swim in his pool.

He took his napkin off his lap and placed it beside his plate. "Well, then, I'll take care of the dishes later—the sun's going to set shortly, so how about we get started?"

THE SKY WAS INCREDIBLE, violet and pink like cotton candy; the Pier was full of life. They could still see it when they got back to the house later, the Ferris wheel lit up in red and green Christmas lights.

Instead of sitting outside with wine, she helped him do the dishes. Then they both checked their phones for flight departure and arrival news. "Still no available seat," he said, "maybe tomorrow afternoon."

"And my friends haven't even gotten to Chicago yet."

"Are you sure you're comfortable if I stay?" he asked, as they were getting ready to say goodnight, to go their separate ways.

"Yes, it's fine. Besides, the knives." She held up her fist as if holding one and made a crazed expression with her eyes.

That laugh of his affected her; it was hard to describe just how, but it melted like honey over her body, soothing and rich and welcome.

She wondered briefly if she had a similar effect on him, but it didn't matter. She wasn't about to dip her toe back in the dating pool, and he would be leaving soon. Besides, he was hot and nice; he surely had a partner.

He gave her his mobile number to put into her phone, "in case you have any questions," he said, and then he scurried off to the pool house. She closed the glass doors behind him and climbed the floating staircase to her suite.

Text messages flew among her friends until it got too late on the east coast.

> Poor you, stuck in that beachfront mansion with a hot single man!

> It's not like that!

> He's cute and sweet but we don't know he's single and anyway, you all know I'm not thinking about that.

She took a bath in the jetted tub, brewed a cup of sleepy tea, watched a movie, read three chapters in her book. And despite it being one in the morning, she could not for anything fall asleep.

When she picked up her phone, a lone text hovered on her locked screen.

> Insomnia strikes. If you're awake and up for a game of air hockey, or cards, pinball, or Marco Polo, I'm a worthy opponent.

> P.S. No need to bring the knives.

> I take it the house (of course!) has a game room. Where exactly is it?

She realized she was smiling while she pulled on her yoga pants and a sweatshirt over her camisole top.

He texted her directions, and he was there waiting in the hall when she arrived.

The game room was unbelievable. It had a glossy basketball-court wooden floor and a hoop and backboard stowed near the ceiling. Arcade machines lined the edge of the room, and against one wall sat a full-size air hockey table.

He followed her to it, switched it on, and by the time they finished, they'd each won a game. Then they lit up the pinball machine, the racket of the bells and the bumpers making them laugh together while they maniacally pressed the flipper buttons.

They played a couple of the other games, fun flashbacks from the eighties, and they each did their best Pac-Man imitations. But at the machine on the end, the one with the black seat and race car steering wheel, he hesitated. A look came over his face like he had taken a punch to the gut, and the happy mood dissipated.

She quickly realized why and took his arm; with her other hand she rubbed his back. "Come on," she whispered as she led him away, "let's go do something else."

He sat at the kitchen island while she made them each a cup of her favorite cocoa, adding a shot of secret-ingredient liqueur and a pinch of kosher salt.

Carefully, they brought the hot, brimming mugs to the terrace. The large chaise lounges were spaced far enough apart that it felt weird not to share one. As they lay in the dark, he talked about his brother, older by two years. He shared memories and how it was now to be without him. She gladly listened, hoping it would help ease his heartbreak. Until sometime during the quiet night, in the darkness laced with the rhythmic surf, they fell asleep side by side, each under their own soft woolly blanket.

They woke at dawn to their phones simultaneously buzzing and chiming. As they rapidly thumbed text message replies, each of them shook their head and sighed.

When they set the phones down and looked at each other, it was with disappointed, sympathetic smiles.

"I'm sorry about your friends," he said. "It looks like it's the two of us for Christmas."

"And I'm sorry you won't be with your family, but I'll prepare us a killer dinner."

"Killer? You're scaring me again," he joked, but her disappointment ballooned. Not only did she desperately want to see her peeps, but the more she looked at him, the more she wondered when, or if, she would be ready to get involved with a man again. She was already forty-nine, but still, imagining a relationship felt so vague and far away. Although the last 18 hours with him might convince her, just maybe, to reconsider.

HE ASKED if he could help with the food, but she told him she had it under control, to do his own thing today. It would be better if they didn't spend too much time together, although that she didn't expressly say.

She put in the earbuds, cranked her tunes, and got lost in her state of flow. Except for when she looked up late afternoon and saw him on the terrace. He sat at the table in front of his laptop, animatedly talking, a video call if she had to guess. But his outfit—she howled with laughter—he was dressed as some kind of loutish anti-Santa.

His fake beard was attached crooked; his glasses sat askew on his nose. Instead of the usual red Santa coat, he wore a tight black motorcycle jacket. Crushed beer cans lay on their sides on the table all around him, and she could tell from how he swayed and moved his mouth that he was purposely acting drunk.

She watched the show for a while, but the food soon needed her attention. When she looked outside the next time, he was no longer there.

A moment later, he came to the doorway of the kitchen, still wearing his rebel-Santa costume and—she was glad to see—a real smile.

"My sister-in-law had said the kids were dreading Christmas, and then there was the weather snafu. So I tried to think of something semi-funny I could do from here. It's hard to cheer up two tweens who no longer believe in Santa and who've had an incredibly shitty year."

"That, my friend, is a very tall order. How did it go?" she asked, although with his sense of humor, she already knew the answer.

The wattage of his slight smile grew, reaching the corners of his eyes. "I think well—at least for the time being —who knows about an hour from now, or tomorrow. But it was great to see them laugh."

"Well, from in here, it looked like a great success." She reached for her phone and asked if she could take his picture. Maybe he'd want it to send to the kids but, also, to be honest, she wanted one for herself.

———

IT WAS dark by the time they sat down to Christmas dinner on the terrace. A few seagulls still drifted in the gentle wind, the squawking more subdued than during the day. Now and then their feathers flashed white as they picked up the glow from the moon. Pool lights shimmied through the water, and a tall outdoor heater removed the chill. The breeze smelled like the sea, hard to discern individual notes but heady when sensed together.

When they finished dessert, second helpings each, he sat back and waved his white cloth napkin. "I surrender," he joked. "It was fantastic and I want more of everything, but I cannot manage another bite."

"I hope you liked it." She could usually tell when people enjoyed her food and when they were faking it, thinking lying was polite. That he seemed to fall into the former camp pleased her. Actually, quite a lot.

"Liked? Did you see how much I ate? I loved it. Part of me hopes I can't fly out tomorrow either, so we can have leftovers."

Him saying "we" had a funny effect, sending a shiver down her body. "I'll pack you a lunch for the flight and, don't worry—"

They said the exact same thing at the exact same time: "No knives." They laughed, but she also felt a pang of sadness at the thought of him not here.

The gulls' squawking soon quieted, and the pier noise slowed to a halt. They sat a little longer, drank the last sips of Cabernet from their glasses. "It's a lovely night," she said, "the air smells so good by the shore."

"I was actually thinking of taking a swim—in the pool, I mean, not the ocean. Would you like to come with?"

She wanted to dive into that shimmering pool so badly, with the warm water and the surface tinkling with moonlight. "Thanks, but that's okay. I think I'll take a walk on the beach instead."

"Okay, sure, I'll go with you." He started to get up. "Wait, sorry—you're probably sick of me crashing your vacation and you want to be alone." He hit his temple with the heel of his hand, like he was a little bit dense.

"No, no, it's not that. It's just . . . I'm not so ready for the pool."

He nodded slowly. "Do you not like the water?"

"I love the water. I used to swim every day. Back in college, I was on the swim team and, actually, one summer I played a mermaid at a quirky theme park. My mom used to say I was part fish."

He laughed but he was thinking, trying to figure it out. "Used to swim, past tense?"

She mm-hm'ed.

"Like in the past, before your surgery?"

She made the same sound again, but the way he looked at her, he was inquiring, and she wanted to tell him. "I actually chose your house for the pool."

His brow pulled in; he didn't comprehend.

"I haven't swam since the surgery. This trip, with my friends, I was going to—forgive the bad pun—dive back in." Her own twist to create some kind of informal but meaningful and needed ritual.

"Don't worry, I'm a sucker for bad puns, but I'm still not sure I understand."

She looked at him self-consciously. "I didn't pack a bathing suit."

"Ohhh, now I'm starting to get it." He feigned a lecherous, eyebrow-waggling look and she couldn't help but laugh, although she had started to feel embarrassed. "So this time with your friends, it would be, like, the first time others would see you swim—skinny dip—after your operation?"

She mm-hm'ed again.

"So bear with me for a second—I'm thinking out loud here. We don't know when your friends will arrive. Hopefully tomorrow, but we're not sure. You love the water, and it's a beautiful night, so it's a shame for you not to go in. What if I leave you alone so you can swim by yourself?"

"No," she answered right away, without thinking, "I don't want you to leave."

Damn, that smile of his.

"Good. That's not my first choice either. So, then, I can stay with you but not look. I can sit over there and look out at the ocean and . . . Wait, I get it." He pretended to whack his temple again. "You need your girlfriends to be with you for this."

Don't cry. "I do."

"Okay—I have an idea. I'll be right back." He jumped up and ran toward his pool house and when he came back to her, he held up three things: A cutoff black tank top; a pair of dark boxer shorts, and. . .

"Is that a shoelace?" she asked.

"It is. You can use it as a belt, to keep the shorts up—they're the smallest I have but they'll still be too big."

"These will work," she said as she took the pieces from him, touched by his thoughtfulness.

He pointed to the cabana. "There are five clean, fluffy robes for all of you in there, and there's a curtain you can pull closed to change. In the meantime, I'll turn up the patio heater, put on my swim trunks, and get us a couple of towels."

HE WAS in the pool at the deep end closest to the ocean when she came out of the cabana, and he didn't look as she got in. Not that there was anything to see, his makeshift bathing suit did the trick—it covered almost everything.

She pushed off the last step and let the warm water draw her in, the tiny bubbles from her motion like fizzy champagne on her skin.

Descending underwater, she swam the length of the pool near the bottom, dragged her fingertips along the pebbled floor. As the water got deeper, the pressure cradled her ears, comforting and familiar. The salt water stung her eyes but not enough to shut them. She wanted to feel it, the pressure, the sting, because they reminded her what she was doing, that she was living her life.

The pool wall was approaching, with two nice legs treading water nearby. She tried not to notice that his body was pretty spectacular up this close. She rose to the surface and shook the dripping water from her smiling face.

"Good?" he asked.

"Wonderful," she sighed.

They swam laps alongside one another and each time she turned her head to inhale a breath, she made sure to watch him move. Finally, when they tired, they took a break in the deep end, resting their forearms on the wall's narrow stone ledge. "Thank you," she said, turning to face him, touching his arm for a second with her hand.

"I didn't do anything, just loaned you a shoelace. But I was wondering—what you went through was a big deal— were you by yourself?"

"Yes and no. My friends, they were amazing from day one, although each was dealing with her own stuff, but otherwise, no. I'm not with anyone; I got divorced several years ago. So those dark thoughts that hit in the middle of the night, the ones you can't turn off? Yes, for those I was alone."

He looked sad, and she could tell it wasn't pity but that he understood. "How about you?" she asked, "Did you have someone with you?"

"When it happened, I was dating a woman, seriously I thought, but then after a couple of months, she complained that I wasn't *present*. The accident, that loss, it was so much, I couldn't figure out how else to be where I was."

"It ended?"

He nodded. "It's a cliché but it really was for the best. You know, you look back and see things you didn't realize or understand at the time."

She shared the story of her lone date, the asshole who left her mid-lunch. "I hope you had your knives with you," he said, and bumped her shoulder.

When she laughed this time, he traced the lower curve of her cheek with his index finger. "When you smile, your cheeks take on this encouraging, optimistic look. I hope it doesn't make you uncomfortable if I say it's really uplifting —and pretty."

"It does a little, but it's okay. It's nice to hear you say it." She held still to let him touch her face. Not only was it nice to hear the words, but his fingertip against her skin was incredibly nice to feel.

"Seriously, that lunch guy? What a fool." He shook his head in disbelief. "You're funny and caring, a totally rad cook, and just a guess from watching you work with your knife—you probably also throw a mean axe."

His humor was dry and offbeat just how she liked it, but her laughter turned to a tremble because the air was cooling down.

"Come on, you're getting cold," he said, and they let go of the ledge, momentarily drifting. Then, with a stroke of their arms in the water, they moved closer to one another. On land they probably would have embraced. But in the pool, their feet without purchase, they were both out of their depth.

The moment passed and they swam to the steps and climbed out of the pool. In the cabana she changed into a fluffy robe, wrung out his wet tank and shorts, draped them over a chair.

When she emerged, he was wearing a similar robe, and he motioned toward their chaise. The remote was in his hand, and he pressed it to turn off the outdoor lights. A slice of moonlight reflected on the ocean and the pool's still surface, but otherwise their terrace was dark.

This time, they shared the same soft, woolly blanket as they talked about a bunch of things and listened to the sounds of the water.

She never would have imagined that a kiss could come about so organically. It seemed like one of them simply turned to the other, both with the same idea, the same desire, at exactly the same time.

His mouth was the perfect balance of salt and sweet, and how the two of them tasted and touched each other was delectable. After a while, she sat up and took a deep breath, then unfastened the belt of her robe. She slid it out from underneath her and set it down on the tile.

He looked at her for a moment, a gorgeous, admiring, moonlit smile dawning on his face. He reached out and brought her close. "You're beautiful," he whispered, "incredibly so. I'd like to touch you, but is that okay? And is there anywhere you don't want me to go?"

"You can touch me everywhere," she said softly against his lips. Kissing them already felt as natural to her as floating in the water.

He moaned her name on his exhale and took her quite literally. He explored her all over with his mouth, slowly, inch by inch. Her lips, her tongue, her earlobes and her neck, her shoulders and her belly, her sides and chest including the scars. Tears tickled her cheek when she realized he had stayed rock-hard against her the entire time.

Like the merman in her dream, he was amply endowed below the waist and he was eager to satisfy. The sex was raw and tender, complete with hushed jokes and laughter. He kissed her and held her tight as she climaxed, which happened twice, she was thrilled to say. The first time took away her self-consciousness, while the second was pure, untainted pleasure. She still needed to swim with her friends nearby, but as she lay against him under the woolly blanket and the stars, she realized she had needed this, too.

IT WASN'T clear what woke them, the dawn light or the buzzing phones. He was finally assigned a flight leaving in a few hours, while her friends texted they were about to take off together from Chicago.

"I'll give you a ride to the airport," she told him as they got up to start their day, a sinking feeling in her belly. Would they see each other again? She would ask the question before they said goodbye, but just in case he said no, she did not want to break the spell just yet.

"Not so fast," he tugged on her hand, "Stay here with me for a second." He laid back down again with her on her side next to him, and she propped herself beside his chest. "This was a wonderful surprise Christmas gift," he said, taking ahold of her face.

"For me also." She stroked the expanse of his broad shoulders.

"Are you free for New Year's?" he asked, "What do you say we spend it together?"

"I'd love that," she replied, stretching up to kiss his lips.

"Great, so it's a date. I didn't rent the house again, so after your friends leave, why don't you just stay?"

She didn't have plans for the rest of the week, and it would be lovely to be here, reminded of him. And—she imagined the feel of bathing in that gorgeous pool—she could swim. "That's so kind, but are you sure it's alright?"

"It's more than alright—I'd like it a lot," he said, looking unsure about sharing more. "Actually, this house? My brother left it to me to take care of until his kids get older. It doesn't seem like mine, that's why I rent it out. But having you here when I get back will make me feel like I've come home."

5

SANTA & BARBARA

In the dream, she was walking through Copenhagen's Nyhavn district, its colorful buildings lining the canal like travel guidebook spines aligned on a tidy shelf. As she crossed the Inner Harbor Bridge, she tightened her trench against the wind as a canal boat glided below. It was one of the long ones that plied the harbor with tourists packed like sardines, the ones that cut the engines to an idle near The Little Mermaid so passengers could snap photos. Only this boat was empty save for one person, a man who looked up at her with a flirty smile, the sexiest gentleman she had ever seen.

Her last relationship had ended badly after several years, with too much anger and sadness and missing. "But that was, what, two years ago?" the man yelled up from the boat as if he could read her mind, "What will it take for you to try again?"

Although it was early December and the boat bobbed in a frosty wind, he started to disrobe. He unzipped his quilted navy-blue jacket, lifted his red tee shirt over his head, turned toward her so she could get a better glimpse of his undulating pecs. And then much to her surprise he unzipped his pants and, voilà, out sprang his manhood at attention.

It was, she could see even from up here on the bridge, quite a considerable size. Not impossibly large or otherwise intimidating; rather, seductive and—she definitely would wager—breathtakingly satisfying.

"Do you see what you do to me?" he called, as if they knew each other well. "Barb, when *will* you be ready?"

Somehow he knew her name but, still, her feelings were conflicted. On one side of the emotional spectrum lay reluctance and self-denial. But on the other—she looked again at his sculpted loins, at the rare December sunlight glinting off the skin at the tip of his member—lay lust, longing, and hunger.

"Jump into the boat," he called, raising his arms into the air. "I'm right here and I'll catch you. We'll have such a great time." But if he missed or dropped her, she knew, she would plunge into the ice-cold water.

It might have been the effect of short winter days, or the threat of a looming solo Christmas in the city known for coziness and *hygge*, but on impulse she decided to jump. She tightened the belt of her coat again, climbed up over the rail, and leapt.

He caught her like he promised, and she took note of the lesson: Not all lovers broke their pledges.

The setting then shifted in a highly surreal way. No longer were they in his boat; somehow they had arrived in his downy bed. He was still naked and—she glanced skyward and mouthed a prayer of thanks—also still ready for action.

Now she was the one to strip and bask in his eager,

unabashed glow. "What do you like?" he asked, "What is it you've been craving?"

"Since you didn't drop me in the water and we're both safe and nice and warm"—she took hold of his erection, felt the heat radiate into her palm—"I'd like this inside me." His smile grew as she straddled his hips and reached back to position him, but he caught her hand mid-air.

"Wait, are you sure you're ready?" he teased, touching his thumb to her swollen bead.

She had grown wet at the first sight of him, the hot guy in his canal boat. "Oh, I'm ready alright," she replied, "Here, I'll show you."

She lowered herself onto him and let out a groaning sigh.

It didn't take long for them to find the perfect tempo, and he held tight to her ass as she bounced. "What were you waiting for?" he asked breathlessly as her wave of pleasure surged toward its crest. "Isn't this worth the risk?"

"Yes, yes, yes," she cried, her voice growing increasingly loud. As the wave hit its peak, she was rendered speechless at the flood of bliss. But then, too soon, just like a real wave, it receded. As she caught her breath, she answered the question he had posed. "It was totally worth it. I wouldn't have wanted to miss out. In fact, when you're ready, let's do it again."

THE LINE WAITING for passport inspection at LAX snaked around the huge space, and she impatiently looked at her watch. The Christmas party at her grandfather's new nursing home—a euphemistically named "memory care center"—was about to start and she still had a two-hour drive. She hadn't been back home to the States or seen him in almost three years and, when a man who's pushing 90 has dementia, she berated herself yet again, that is an awfully long time.

"He's gotten a lot worse," her older brother Jake had told her on the phone several months ago, before the facility switch. "They found him one night lost and wandering the parking lot. And last time I was there, Barb, it was terrible. He didn't know who I was." She could hear the sadness in Jake's voice as he told her the doctors said they should move him, and it made her chest feel leaden. So she had glanced at her watch and employed her usual defense mechanism: She told him she was meeting a tour group, which wasn't a lie, and needed to get going.

Jake visited their grandfather often and oversaw his care. Since she lived a continent away she had a convenient excuse not to be as involved, or—she covered her mouth with her palm and shook her head—rarely even there. It was true that she was busy with her Copenhagen tour business, leading cycle trips around the city, taking customers on private canal boat tours and through Tivoli Gardens. But the real reason, she could barely admit the ugly truth to herself, was that her grandfather had been the father she didn't have growing up, and it was gut-wrenchingly painful to watch his decline close up.

This year, though, Jake wanted to spend Christmas with his new partner's family, and Barb knew he needed a break. But she couldn't let Morfar—she and Jake called him by the Danish word—spend Christmas in his new nursing home alone.

"Welcome home," the border control agent said as he handed Barb back her blue passport. She stuck it hastily in her bag and hurried to the customs area. Once her bag was through the scanner, she rushed to the pickup spot and waited under a sign that read, Car Rental Shuttles.

In the convertible she had reserved, she cruised along the 101 through Silver Lake and into the Hollywood Hills, then west toward Thousand Oaks and Ventura. The mountains and, when she finally hit the coast, the scent of the saltwater air—they helped to calm her jitters, a helpful arrival gift.

She found the memory care center, parked the convertible in the lot, and glanced at the clock on the dashboard as she got out. The party was scheduled to end in a half-hour. Guilt again began to tug at her gut, even as part of her was grateful she had been delayed. He was surely having fun; after all, Christmas had been his very favorite thing. So wouldn't it be even better for the two of them to visit later, or tomorrow, when all the festivities were done?

For as long as she could remember, every Christmas Morfar had dressed up as Santa and rode his Harley in the Solvang Danish Christmas festival parade. Solvang was their adopted hometown after they moved in the 1950s from Copenhagen. Barb's grandmother would dress as Mrs. Claus and ride on the bike behind him, her laughing smile continuous, her arms tight around his padded waist, while Barb rode in the sidecar dressed up like a *nisse*, playing a Nordic elf.

She paused by the big potted palm just outside the nursing home's glass entry doors to steel herself and take a breath. But there must have been an overeager motion sensor because they slid open to suck her inside before she felt remotely ready.

At the receptionist's call, Morfar's social worker came to the front desk to greet her. "We've been telling him you're coming, but you might have to re-introduce yourself. You'll find him down the hall"—she gestured—"the community room is to the left." Then the counselor gave Barb an understanding look that she didn't believe she deserved. She felt like a selfish shit; she had put off making this visit for far too long.

THE PARTY in the community room was still in full swing when she got to the doorway. The scent of cloves and cinnamon, fresh-baked cookies, and the sounds of music from the sixties filled the air. A chuckle broke through her nerves and guilt at the sight of the Elvis impersonator. Dressed in a tight white shirt and matching bell bottoms, with a slick black pompadour and dark sunglasses too, he thrust his hips impressively as he crooned. People were up and dancing near the platform that served as a stage—from the spread in ages it must be staff and residents alike. Laughing and dancing up a storm together, using their walkers, wheelchairs, and canes.

She looked around the crowd, up there having a great time but Morfar wasn't among them. Then she turned and scanned the tables on the other side of the space, each with a small decorated tree at the center. There, in the back, at a table by himself sat a man with a doleful expression. It looked like Morfar but not really. Her heart felt tight and heavy, like it might actually drop and break. This is exactly why she had stayed away. Gaunt and frail, and his eyes—even from her safe doorway, she could tell they had dimmed.

He might not remember her or their connection; he might not know her name, that's what Jake and the social worker had said. There was nothing she could do to improve his situation, and seeing him like this, well, coming here clearly was a mistake. The irony didn't escape her—he had always been proud that his roots were in Scandinavia, where people really looked out for each other. She took a step backward into the hallway so now just her head peeked around the wall. She could back out as easily as she had come in, return later when it was a more opportune time. Maybe by then he'd feel better. In the meantime, she could take a drive, muster more strength, restitch her aching heart.

But as she turned to leave, she felt someone at her back. When she turned to look, it was a man dressed as Santa. But he reminded her, in both stature and how he had caught her sneaking, of a bouncer. His face was obscured by a fake white beard and thick sideburns, but she could see that his skin was supple. His build and the buzz cut underneath his red hat also told her that he was not of old Santa age—no, he was probably closer to hers, give or take around forty-five.

His kind eyes and what he said pierced her plans, a hairpin to a balloon: "You must be Barb, the granddaughter flying in from Copenhagen."

"That would be me," she said, sheepishly extending her hand to meet his. Maybe it was her guilty conscience, but she had a funny feeling he knew damn well she had just been about to bolt.

"I'm one of the social workers here—not your grandfather's, although I know him. But today, I'm moonlighting. Obviously" —he pointed at his costume—"as Santa. Why don't we go and see him?"

ELVIS JUMPED OFF HIS STAGE, twisting and weaving toward the residents who had stayed at their tables.

His lavalier mic meant both of his hands were free. When he stopped by each person, he gently swung their arms to the music so they were dancing in their seats.

Next, Elvis headed to a few residents in the back row who looked not-so-enthusiastic. He stopped by her grandfather's table and placed a hand on Morfar's back, bent over to whisper something near his ear, but Morfar only shook his head. Who had she been kidding, there was no way in hell she could leave.

As if he could see her thinking, Santa's hand went to her lower back and his encouraging touch nudged her forward. "It's hard to watch him like this, I know. But once he sees you, he'll probably feel better." Then as if still reading her mind he added, "If he doesn't seem to remember, or even if he stays quiet or gets agitated, I believe some inner part of him will know you're here."

"It helps when you frame it that way," she said, resolving to commit what he said to long-term memory.

Before they got to Morfar though, Santa excused himself and went to speak to another resident. When he sat down beside the woman, she positively beamed and took ahold of his hand. Barb of course had no idea, but she imagined he reminded her of a son or grandson—someone, clearly, she loved.

Alone, she made her way to Morfar, who was staring into space. She held her breath as she got closer, paused beside him to see how he would react. He turned and when he saw her, his eyes suddenly brightened. His smile, too, it lit his face and straightaway stole her angst.

"Nisse! You came," he exclaimed, remembering her nickname no less, and she leaned down to give him a hug and kiss. His shoulders were bonier than the last time she had visited him at the previous nursing home, and when he raised his arms to embrace her, they ever so slightly shook.

"I came, Morfar, so we could spend Christmas." She knelt by his side, and although she felt tears well, she tried hard not to cry.

"It's wonderful to see you, darling. You're looking so well. How are things in Copenhagen?"

His recall seemed spot on, and she felt immense relief. It wasn't a mistake for her to come; he recognized her, and he was so pleased.

"Things in Copenhagen are great—the tours are going really well. I take visitors to Tivoli almost every day—remember the vintage cars, and the music carousel?"

Shit! She had told herself so many times not to ask him if he remembered anything. She had read that online in countless articles, and she and Jake had talked about it a million times. But reminiscing came so naturally, especially with him, that the question just slipped out.

"You always insisted on riding in an ivory car, and only the ones with the red seats," he answered.

"I had forgotten about that—that's right. I would ask you to let the people behind us go first so I could wait for the right car."

He laughed at that and nodded. "Oh, Nisse, honey, where did the time go?"

"I don't know, Morfar—it's flown so fast. How are you doing here? And how are you enjoying the party?"

"It's a fine place, and the party was splendid, but we should get ready to leave. Your grandmother's at home preparing your lunch. I promised her we wouldn't be late; she cannot wait to see you."

Her lungs deflated at his words, although she had known to expect this—the jumps in time, the confusion amid lucidity, lucidity amid the confusion, thinking the past was still present tense. But no preparation was enough to stop the twister of feelings at experiencing it firsthand.

Something made her turn, and she noticed Santa glance in her direction. Those eyes of his, they were saying something but what exactly she couldn't read. Maybe, if she hadn't been so checked out, avoidant the past few years, her receiver would be better tuned. But what she did get from his expression was a warm rush of understanding and support.

Morfar was asking more questions, now one about college and her internship in Denmark. It had been close to 25 years ago, so she decided to tell him the story he used to know.

"Great, the internship was great," she said. "I came home to finish school and then decided to go back after graduation. I started my own tour business, and it's been doing really well. That's why I go to Tivoli and get to see the vintage cars all the time. They look so small now, it's funny."

She didn't add anything about her grandmother, who was not home preparing lunch. She had died three years ago —Barb's last visit to the States was for her funeral. For Morfar, a loss after being married almost 50 years was hard enough to survive once. Forgetting and being told anew would only make the pain echo too many times.

"Well, it's wonderful to hear how well you're doing, Nis. Your grandmother and I are just so happy you've come home."

"I'm happy I've come home too, Morfar." Still kneeling beside him, she rubbed his back and from behind him saw Santa approach.

"Barb, let me get you a chair." He returned a moment later and set the seat down beside her grandfather.

"Thanks," she said, "I think my knees were about to give out." When Santa laughed all throaty, she started to feel lightheaded. Maybe it was good she was about to take a seat.

Elvis hopped back onto the stage and picked up his guitar. He said something about playing his favorite Christmas song and strummed the first few notes as his band started up behind him. The song was "Blue Christmas," and it felt like a fist slammed into her chest. She could vividly picture Morfar and Mormor dancing to it in their Solvang living room.

The music stirred something in Morfar too because he smiled wistfully, and his eyes grew moist. "Your grandmother and I loved this song—we danced to it every Christmas Eve."

"I know, Morfar," she said, gently lifting the piece of hair that had fallen onto his forehead. "I can picture you two in the living room—I can still see the golden-brown shag carpeting and the wood paneling on the wall. What do you say—I'm not Mormor, but shall we dance?"

He looked at her and then he shifted his gaze to Santa, who was still standing beside them. "No thanks, Nisse," Morfar said. "These days I have two left feet, but you love to dance—why don't you dance with Santa?"

"Santa's busy, Morfar." She hated how condescending it sounded as she said it, like talking down to a child, or someone who didn't speak the language. But when she looked at Santa for backup, he only reached out his beefy arm to take her hand.

"While Elvis plays, it's my duty today to engage the residents and their guests," Santa said, while she tried not to think about those arms around her body. "If I dance with you, it looks like I accomplish both those aims, so you're helping me do my job." He nodded toward Morfar, who sat back in his chair with a guiltily innocent smile.

She only took Santa's hand for Morfar's sake, went with him toward the stage and danced to that Elvis song. It wasn't for the feeling of his arm around her, or of holding his hand, or of her cheek against his chest. And it was definitely not for the feeling that she could relax into that body of his as if it were a cushy couch.

They moved together easily, gliding with the rhythm of the music. Their bodies fit together like two pieces of a puzzle and . . . wait, no. Something might be rising in his red pants. He cleared his throat and took a small step back to create more distance between them.

The thought she had at that moment was completely inappropriate for a family-oriented holiday party. For goodness' sake, was she shameless, having lewd thoughts about Santa, the social worker? She may have been the owner of a healthy if not frustrated libido but, she reminded herself, she was here for only one reason.

When she looked over at Morfar, he was still smiling that impish smile, proof he was trying to fix her up. That smile flipped back the years like animated calendar pages, reminding her of the past—their trips to Copenhagen when she was a child, her visits to him and Mormor in Solvang during her college breaks, the two of them beaming each year on their motorcycle in the Julefest parade.

"Hey, I have an idea," she said, patting Santa's muscular shoulder. Why hadn't she thought of this before? "Can you help me borrow a wheelchair?"

"YOU CAN'T TAKE HIM OUT," the designated social worker said as she and Morfar and Santa congregated by the front desk. "I mean, it's not expressly forbidden but it's not a good idea. First, there's the rarity of your visit—it's been a *very* long time since he's seen you—and then an outing? He's bound to get disoriented."

"He's already disoriented," she answered, although she knew it could get a lot worse. This idea of hers, granted it might be reckless and irresponsible, but she knew in her heart and without any doubt, he would want to experience it—revive the old memories or create new ones, however long they might last.

She straightened her shoulders and looked the woman in the eye. "I'm here now," she continued, "and I'm willing to take that chance."

The woman looked uncomfortable; she eyed Barb with disdain. "Would you like to confer with your brother? I'll call him, since he's the one who's usually . . ."

Here.

"That won't be necessary. I suspect Jake," who had just taken a leap of his own to start a relationship with his new girlfriend, Ava, "would agree. But regardless of whether he's on board or not, please, I'd like a wheelchair for my grandfather."

WITH MORFAR IN HIS WINDBREAKER, she wheeled him out the institutional glass doors, down the ramp, and across the parking lot.

When they got to her rental car with the convertible top still down, she pulled up the Julefest website on her phone.

The parade, it turned out was actually today, and that coincidence was a true gift. But as she bent to put his feet on the ground and help him into the front seat, he gripped the chair's armrests and jerked back. "Where are you taking me? I can't go with you—only my wife can sign me out."

She let go of his foot and knelt before him. With the stoop of his shoulders, now they were almost at eye level. "No, I'm not your wife, Morfar. It's me, Nisse, your . . ." *Granddaughter. Please remember.*

He hung his head for a moment and when he lifted it again slightly, dismay and frustration filled his eyes. "Nisse. I'm sorry. I—" he hesitated, searched for words "—sometimes I get things mixed up."

She breathed a sigh of relief. "Don't apologize, Morfar. Sometimes I get things mixed up too. But today I was thinking we could do something really special—we could go to the Julefest, see what's going on. If we hurry, we might be able to make the parade."

"Wonderful idea, Nis—I love it. And after, we can get *æbleskiver* with cherry sauce—this year your beautiful grandmother is working the booth."

Her heart sank anew. What in the North Pole was she supposed to say? Her only hope was that by the time they got to the festival, about 45 minutes away, he would forget this part of the mission.

By now she had helped him into the car, got him situated in the front seat. Just as she tugged the seat belt to extend around him, she heard a man's deep voice call, "Wait, don't leave yet, Barb."

Santa ran across the lot, a tote bag swinging from his fist. "You said he used to dress as Santa every year, so I thought he might need this. Although officially"—he cleared his throat—"I'm supposed to think it's a bad idea for him to leave."

She could feel her face pucker with confusion but then break into a smile. He held up the bag with one hand and with the other showed her the contents as he explained. "I'm donating my beard; one of the nurses shared her red hat; and here—take my Santa jacket."

She stood there agog, so touched she didn't know what to say. "Thank you, wow," she managed, "that's amazing."

"Nisse, hurry," Morfar said from the car. "We don't want to miss the parade. Your grandmother will be waiting."

She took a deep breath and looked at Santa for some kind of confirmation. Maybe this outing really was a mistake; she felt so fickle and ill-equipped. One minute she hoped Morfar would remember; a second later, she willed him to forget.

"Here take my number," Santa quickly said. "Call or text if you have any trouble."

THEY ARRIVED downtown just as the afternoon parade was about to start rolling, and by some stroke of luck joined the end of the line. "Now, let's put on your Santa costume." She shifted the car into park, hopped out, and dashed around to his side.

She put the jacket and the beard and hat on him, and then she got back in.

They motored along Mission and Copenhagen Drive, and he smiled and waved non-stop. His ho-ho-ho sounded jolly although his voice quivered with age. Along both sides of the route, people cheered and waved. All the kids and the laughter—no question, this was what he loved, all these happy faces.

When they got to the end of the route and the parade disbanded, he sighed deeply, looking happy but exhausted. After a moment he turned to face her. "Nisse, that was the most fun I've had in a long time. I can't thank you enough."

She leaned in and gently kissed his cheek, took a hold of his thin hand. "That was the most fun *I've* had in a long time—since you used to take me in the sidecar in fact—and I can't thank *you* enough."

"Hah! You still remember that?" he asked, which made her grin. "We had a ball back then, didn't we?"

She had almost said, 'Of course I remember,' but memory wasn't a given. Instead she said, "I can see it in my mind like it was yesterday—those were wonderful memories you gave me."

He squeezed her hand and looked out the windshield at the half-timbered buildings with their copper roofs. Then he turned to her again and asked, "So, Nis, is there anyone special in your life?"

Morfar had met her ex years ago, and this she was relieved he didn't remember. "Not at the moment," she said. "Life keeps me busy, between a lot of good friends and the tour business and . . . Oh, I brought some pictures to show you," she remembered, "We can look at them tomorrow and you can see how the city has changed since you left."

He nodded slowly, thinking, and then smiled as if he hit on a solution. "Say, let's hurry and get back. There's someone I want you to meet."

THE GROUCHY social worker was gone for the day when she and Morfar returned. The evening staff let her stay for dinner and to help him get ready for bed. She tucked him in and moved the guest chair closer. The two of them recited "'Twas the Night Before Christmas" just like they used to when she was a child, only this time she was the one who helped fill in the missing words.

There was no more denying the truth of his situation, no matter how far away she stayed. He had changed so much, and other than calls and letters, she had not been present. Her distance might have been protective in some ways, but it had left gaps in both their lives.

"I'm so sorry I haven't seen you at Christmas the last few years." A sob formed somewhere in her chest, and she caught it in her throat. She wouldn't stuff her feelings away anymore, but the last thing she wanted now was to upset him.

"Don't give it a second thought, Nis," he replied and waved his hand. "You're here now, that's what counts. Besides, you've given me a marvelous gift."

She kept the tears at bay as she leaned over and kissed his forehead, turned off his bedside lamp. "I'll be here bright and early tomorrow and we'll spend the day together. Sweet dreams."

"Sweet dreams," he said and squeezed her hand again, his strength diminished from what she remembered.

The sob she had stifled, and many more like it, erupted the second she slipped from his room. She closed the door tight, leaned against the wall, and quietly let them come.

When she happened to look up, there was Santa, in plain clothes, coming down the hall. He stood next to her and opened his arms, and it might have been crazy but she stepped into them without a second thought.

"It's hard to watch this process," he whispered as he held her. She nodded her agreement against him. "I know you feel bad because it's been a long time since you saw him," he went on, "but you're here now, and you made him really happy today."

She sniffled before she spoke. "That's almost word for word what he said."

"We say that kind of sappy stuff a lot around here." The playful look he gave her made her laugh at the very same time she cried.

"Thanks for the Santa accessories—I think they helped him remember. Even if he forgets again tomorrow."

"Exactly, and you're welcome. I was happy to support the cause." There was that sweet, playful look again, and she decided to stop crying.

Gently, he moved her away and put his hands on her shoulders. "Barb, can I ask, where are you staying while you're here?"

"At one of the hotels downtown. When my grandmother died, we sold their house."

"Well, here's an idea. Come out to my place—I live in Carpinteria. We can have a drink or take a walk on the beach. And you're welcome to stay the night instead of in a hotel. It's not a proposition; I'll sleep on the couch. But it might be easier for you than being alone."

"It's funny, but being alone has been easier than the alternative these last few years, but I think I'm ready to change that. A walk on the beach sounds perfect—I've missed the sounds and the smell of the Pacific."

She followed him in her car and chuckled at the street sign at the corner by his house.

"No joke, you live on Santa Claus Lane?" she asked when they got out.

"No joke," he said, opening the door to a retro A-frame cottage. She changed into her sneakers and put on a sweater since the air had cooled down. They crossed the train tracks to the wide, moonlit beach and walked near the edge of the surf.

At one point, the backs of their hands bumped and instead of moving further apart, they simply laced their fingers together. They walked for a while longer, until he stopped and turned to face her. "I meant what I said earlier —tonight wasn't a proposition. But I also want to say that I wasn't only trying to be kind. I felt something—a spark, a connection—as soon as I saw you today at the party. And not to sound like I'm building a case, but I think your grandfather noticed it too."

His smile was utterly endearing, with a hefty dose of sultry. She remembered their dance this afternoon—how he'd started to get hard, how she'd wanted him then and there. "That makes three of us," she said, pitching up on her toes to get closer to his lips.

They kissed softly at first, then harder as the waves crashed against the shore. "Let's go back," she whispered after they'd been at it a while. She wanted to undress him, feel his body against hers—this time without any Santa Claus clothes.

His bed was as soft and downy as the stranger's in her dream and as they lay naked pressed together, he asked, "What do you like, Barb? Tell me what you need."

It didn't take long for them to find the perfect tempo, and he held tight to her ass the whole time. As her wave of pleasure hit its peak, she was rendered speechless, not only by the flood of bliss but also again by the realization. She had been so focused on protecting herself from danger that she had deprived herself of too much.

Maybe what she was doing here with him was reckless and irresponsible; maybe it wouldn't survive beyond tonight. But she knew in her heart and without any doubt, she wanted to experience it—to heal old hurtful recollections and create new ones, however long they would last.

LET'S STAY IN TOUCH!

Want to stay up to date on new releases? Just add your email to my list. I usually email only a few times a year. E-newsletter content includes

- Brief updates and links to new blog posts (often, book recs)
- Early access to free advance review copies
- Bonus content and subscriber-only previews of new work

Are you in? I hope so. As an indie author, I so appreciate readers who want to stay connected. Thank you. 🙏

ALSO BY TALYA BLAINE

CALIFORNIA DREAMS SERIES

California Dreams Christmas Romance Collection
(short stories)

"...a delightful read, perfect for the holiday season...an ideal read for a lazy afternoon." (*NetGalley reviewer*)

Spice level: 🌶️🌶️ to 🌶️🌶️🌶️ / 5

Santa and Anna Christmas Cookie Crash (a novel)

"It's warm, hopeful, and just a little bit magical, the way the best holiday stories always are." (Literary Titan)

"Sugar, spice, and everything nice are the main ingredients in this cozy holiday romance." (Publishers Weekly Booklife Prize)

Spice level: 🌶️🌶️ / 5

TRANSFORMATION SERIES

"Wow! Wow! Wow! The first truly believable BDSM series I have read...a serious, deeply sensual exploration of desire, written expertly and sensitively... These two characters have been crafted to perfection...you'll never be able to forget them." -Goodreads reviewer

Silently (Book 1)

"the new 50 Shades" (*NetGalley reviewer*)

Spice level: 🌶️🌶️🌶️🌶️ / 5

Secretly (Book 2)

Publishers Weekly BookLife Prize quarter-finalist

Spice level: 🌶️🌶️🌶️🌶️ / 5

Entirely (Book 3)

"as tender as it is steamy..." (*NetGalley reviewer*)

Spice level: 🌶️🌶️🌶️🌶️ / 5